GRADUATION DETONATION

MIDDLE SCHOOL MAYHEM BOOK TWELVE

C.T. WALSH

FARCICAL PRESS

COVER CREDITS

Cover design by Books Covered
Cover photographs © Shutterstock
Cover illustrations by Maeve Norton

For my Family

Thank you for all of your support

1

I t was time to move on. Time to grow up. Time to maturely egg your rival's house during spirit week. Time to graduate. Moving on. Moving up. Lots of ons and ups. And if you've been paying attention, you'll know that there will also be quite a few downs and a tad bit of mayhem along the way. Or heaping piles of it. (You'll find that funnier later.)

My name is Austin Davenport and this is my story about the final weeks of my life. In middle school. I should probably make that clear. That was a bit too ominous. I apologize. This isn't one of those stories where the hero dies in the end. I come close a few times, but I want to make it known right from the get-go given the title of this story about detonation- no people, real or written, died or were blown up in the making of this story. Not even Randy Warblemacher. Sorry about that. But still, you *will* be blown away!

This story begins on the first day back at school after our class trip disaster, where I, and all of my classmates, actually nearly died. Can you actually nearly die? I believe you can. And I did. Actually nearly. Anyway, the parents of the eighth-grade class at Cherry Avenue Middle School were livid. Normally, middle school students embellish a little from time to time (not me, of course), but everything that was said about our trip was true. We did actually nearly starve, drown, get eaten by a bear, and trampled by a moose stampede. A few people ate poison berries. Our teacher got bitten by a venomous snake. You get the drift. It was not a kumbaya experience filled with cozy campfires and s'mores.

Somebody's dad called the news in anger. Somebody who didn't actually watch our local news. Channel 2 did what they always did. They sent Calvin Conklin, the worst local newsman in the history of the news, to our school. I wasn't sure if it was a proven fact that he was the worst, but the anecdotal evidence was pretty obvious if you just watched one of his interviews.

The school had a love-hate relationship with Channel 2. They were often invited to our school events to heap praise on our principals and when they did that, the school loved them. But when the school was under fire and subject to Channel 2 highlighting Cherry Avenue's many deficiencies like the death toll from the corrosive casserole, Calvin was not allowed on school property. But since I had to walk from the high school to the middle school after my high school science class (I'm pretty smart), I had to pass Calvin and his camera crew, who were filming just outside the middle school entrance.

I took a deep breath when I saw Calvin. I hadn't had any good experiences with him through the years, but I was still angry about the class trip. I had some things I wanted to say. Our principal, Ms. Ann Pierre, commonly known as Ms. Armpit Hair, needed to be fired.

I walked along the fence, heading toward the entrance. Calvin's eyes lit up as he saw me.

Calvin said, "This kid looks like he needs some attention. I'm sure he can be exploited for our evil corporate purposes." Calvin put his finger to his earpiece. "What's that, Ted? I'm not supposed to reveal our sinister plans to rule the world by manipulating the masses? Nobody told me that! I just posted that on Instagram. Ted, how many followers do I have? Only ten thousand? How many does that idiot weatherman, Storm Waters have? What? Oh, right. Hey kid!"

Calvin hustled over to me and thrust the microphone in my face. "Why do you look familiar, kid?"

I wasn't going to tell him about all the times we had crossed paths. "You've probably just seen me around. You've done a lot of stories here."

"I have, haven't I?"

"Yes, that's why I said it." I was already regretting the interview.

"Please, just a few questions," Calvin said.

I nodded. "Just as long as they're about the class trip."

Calvin looked like I insulted his mother. "Of course, they will be. I never go off topic." Calvin pressed his earpiece. "Ted, maybe we should do a 'Through the Years' piece on Cherry Avenue. You really think that's a great idea?" Calvin asked, excitedly. "My mom is gonna be so proud. Oh, we're on?" So much for staying on topic.

Calvin cleared his throat and looked back at the camera. "Class trip gone horribly wrong. Kids lost at sea. Almost nearly drowned. Starving. A bear attack. Big Foot. Diarrhea." Calvin spoke to Ted again, "Ted, did Big Foot *have* diarrhea? I bet that was pretty nasty. Oh, right. Calvin looked back at the camera and spoke, "Horrible campfire songs. A moose stampede." Calvin touched his earpiece again. "Ted, is it meese or moose?" He looked at me. "Do you know? Ted doesn't have a clue."

I quickly realized I had made a mistake by agreeing to the interview. "There's no story here."

"It's not a story. It's an exposé," Calvin said.

"I don't know what that is."

"Me, neither. Ted, what's an exposé again?"

I shook my head and pushed past Calvin. A burly school security guard was heading toward me, a concerned look on his face. It was the first time I was happy to see him or any of his brethren. They were normally chasing me or at least eyeing me with disapproval. I got my first security guard escort that was not supposed to end with me in the principal's office.

"Let's get you out of here," the security guard said in a deep voice. "I can't stand that guy. Do you know he had the nerve to talk about my unibrow on live TV? My kids saw that, man."

"He's the worst," I said, as we headed into the school. "Nobody listens to him anyway. He was talking about Big Foot's diarrhea."

"Why does he always have to talk about people's personal matters?"

I didn't know how to answer that, being that Big Foot is not actually a person, and perhaps not even real, so I just shrugged and said, "Thanks for the help."

"Any time." He looked down at me, his demeanor changing. He furrowed his unibrow. "Now get to class," he said, sternly. I guessed that since I was safe from the evil clutches of the media, things were back to normal.

I shrugged and headed to my Advisory class. I slipped

into my seat next to Just Charles just as the Speaker of Doom crackled to life for the morning announcements.

It was Ms. Armpit Hair herself. She didn't often do the morning announcements. She only graced us with her presence when she wanted to exact less-than-deserved justice on me or defend her actions to the masses. "Good morning!" she said, more cheerful than I had ever heard her. "I hope everyone had a *spectacular* weekend. Despite a little drizzle and a whole lot of embellishment, the eighth-grade class trip to Rocky River was a massive success. Our students came back with new wisdom and life experience that they will carry with them for the rest of their lives."

"More like nightmares," I said, to laughter.

"This lady is a nut job," Just Charles said.

Kami Rahm asked, "Do you think she'll get fired for the class trip?"

Just Charles said, "My dad doesn't think so. Just bad luck."

"Bad luck? We almost died," I said.

"That's too bad. She should be fired," Kami said.

"Who cares? We're outta here in a few weeks," Just Charles said.

"And then we have four years of Butt Hair," I added. I was talking about our former middle school principal who had been transferred to the high school after he and I battled. And I won.

Just Charles said, "I should ask my dad what it's like. He's had like thirty years of butt hair."

"My dad has a lot of butt hair, too."

"What are you talking about?" Kami Rahn asked.

"Butt hair," I said, simply. "Are you looking forward to it?"

Kami rolled her eyes. "Ugh. I can't wait until high school.

I can talk to mature men and not dumb middle school boys."

I chuckled. She was going to be sorely disappointed. My sister was in high school and the boys that came around were certainly not mature. Yeah, they may have had better mustaches than the middle school kids, but they still farted, burped, and discussed butt hair during most meals and family gatherings. And they could even have butt hair, for all I knew. It would be new for them, so maybe they needed to talk about butt hair even more than middle schoolers did.

Ms. Armpit Hair continued with the morning announcements. "And onto bigger and better things. Let's leave the class trip behind like it never happened. And anyone who brings it up will be flogged."

"What the heck is flogged?" Just Charles said, scratching his head.

"Doesn't sound good," I responded.

"It is now time to announce our two finalists for this year's eighth-grade class's valedictorian," Ms. Armpit Hair said, a lot less enthused than when she was trying to talk us into how wonderful the actually nearly deadly class trip was.

I straightened up. I had almost forgotten. I was surely going to be in the running. I wasn't surprised. I was the only kid in middle school taking high school classes.

Ms. Armpit Hair said, "Randolph Warblemacher is our first candidate."

Nearly my whole class groaned. Actually.

"And-" A deep breath echoed through the Speaker of Doom. "Austin Davenport," she said, glumly. There may have even been some retching. "The valedictorian will be announced on stage at the graduation ceremony and will be dependent on these fine (more retching) students' grade point averages."

"Nice work, bro!" Just Charles said. "You have to take Randy down."

"It is what it is. We only have finals left. Most of it's already decided from three years' worth of grades."

"Still. He needs to be crushed."

The announcements continued, "We will also have a student fundraiser this Saturday. It's our annual carnival day. All the local elementary school children will join us for a fun day of festivities that we will charge them dearly for. It's amazing how much parents will pay to keep their kids quiet and entertained."

Jay Parnell said, "We're always raising money for the school, but we never see any of it."

"That's not true," Mrs. Callahan said.

I defended Jay. "This place is falling apart. Zorch can't put enough duct tape on stuff."

"Oh, you've always been a great storyteller, Austin."

Mrs. Callahan sat down on her chair, which promptly toppled over, the faux metal support snapping in two. She collapsed to the floor with a cheap clank and a scream. A few kids laughed while others helped Mrs. Callahan up.

"I'm sick of this place!" she yelled, kicking the leg of her desk, which popped clean off and helicoptered across the floor. "Ms. Pierre is stealing from the school!"

I wasn't convinced she was stealing from the school. Just a poor allocator of resources.

Mrs. Callahan continued her diatribe, "There are three statues of her around the school and she's always going to administrator conferences in exotic places! Hawaii. Bali. Iceland. A bunch of places in Thailand that I can't pronounce. I can't even get a chair that doesn't break!"

One thing was clear. Mrs. Callahan was at her own breaking point. With only days left in school, I think most teachers were at that point. They were like zombies walking down the halls. Bloodshot eyes. Unkempt hair. Double fisted with coffee. It's the mayhem. And it was only just beginning. Dun, dun, dunnnnn....

2

I was in Hell. Otherwise known as gym class. I stood on the baseline of the basketball court, surrounded by my nerd friends.

"I can't believe you're going to be valedictorian, dude," Ben said. He threw his fist in the air. "Nerd power!"

"Shhh," I said. "Don't say it too loud. We don't want the athletes to know we're going to rule them one day."

"Oh, right."

Randy entered the gym and passed by our group with laughter. "Hey, Davenfart! What does it feel like to be second best?"

"I don't know, Randolph. You'll find out when I beat you out for valedictorian."

Randy chuckled. "In your dreams."

"I assure you, I don't dream about you."

Randy ran his fingers through his hair. "You'd be one of the few not to."

The kid was unbelievable. I admired his confidence, though, misguided as it was.

Randy added, "Your girlfriend does."

I wished my nerd power extended to my fists, but at least it covered my words. "The girlfriend who dumped you and came back to me?" I said, nearly puking. The whole idea of Randy having dated Sophie, however brief and misguided, sickened me, but I couldn't pass up the chance to stick it to Randy's ego. It was far more harmful to him than it was to me.

"Whatever. I'm gonna crush you, Davenfart. You've always been second best with your brother. Now you're second best with me."

Mr. Muscalini approached us. "Second best? We don't accept second best in Gopherville!"

Ben whispered to me, "Does he think Gopherville is a real town?"

I shrugged. "I think it is to him. He might live here. There's a shower in the locker room and he's got about a ton of protein powder in his office. He could live here for years."

Mr. Muscalini continued, "Haven't I taught you anything?"

"No," Alex Chu said, and then pointed at Kevin Lynch with a surprised look on his face. A bunch of us chuckled.

Mr. Muscalini shook his head, disappointed. "In just a few short weeks, you'll be moving on to bigger and better things. Leaving me behind. While you can't take your favorite teacher with you, don't leave behind the many great life lessons I taught you." He looked around at each of us. "But you can take pictures of my biceps and upload them to social media. Hashtag- beast-ceps. I can't believe these monsters haven't trended yet." He looked at his biceps and smiled.

I chuckled. I was surprised hearts didn't start floating around everywhere as he gazed at his masterpieces.

"Let's discuss some of those life lessons now," Mr.

Muscalini said. "Everybody repeat after me. Sky's out..." We all joined in. "Thighs out." "Sun's out?"

I yelled, "Buns out!"

Everybody except Randy laughed. Even Mr. Muscalini chuckled. "Only if the beach is empty." He looked at Ben. "Gordo! What's the most important lesson of all?"

Ben shifted back and forth on his feet. "Umm, dodgeball is life, sir?"

"Is that a question, Gordo?"

"No, sir! Dodgeball is life, sir!"

"Good man. You might only get your butt kicked on B days in high school, Gordo. Impressive for someone of your stature and athletic ability."

Ben gave him a less-than-hearty thumbs up.

"Coach, can we play dodgeball one last time?" Randy asked.

"Kiss up," I whispered.

"He's not kissing up. He just wants to crush us one last time," Ben said.

Mr. Muscalini's eyes appeared to tear up. He tried to speak, but couldn't. He nodded and turned his back on us.

Randy looked over at me and smirked. He mouthed, "You might not dream about me, but I'm gonna be in your nightmares."

Gulp.

The game started soon enough. Sweat dripping. Pulses pounding. Fear swarming. And that was before Mr. Muscalini blew the whistle. As the traumatic chirp blasted our ear drums, all of the athletes surged toward the middle of the gym, ammunition on their minds.

Randy had his eyes on me, but I was way ahead of him. I yelled out, "Nerd herd!"

Everyone crowded around me, protecting me. By

combining the entrepreneurial concepts of the first-mover advantage and the network effect, people joined my nerd herd first, and rather than build their own, others took advantage of one that was already built.

I was face to face with Ben, as the nerd herd spun around. The most effective nerd herd, besides getting into the middle as soon as possible, was to hold onto each other and spin slowly. That way, we held each other up, and nobody got beaned repeatedly. You have a whole rotation for your pain to subside.

I said, "Hey, man. How's it going?"

Ben frowned, "I'm going to miss this."

"You are?" I asked, surprised.

"Well, no, but maybe we could build a fort together over the summer and hang out in it or something."

"There is something comforting about hanging out with you guys in close spaces," Jay Parnell said from the outer ring of the herd.

"That's weird, dude," I said.

"That hurts, bro!" Jay said.

"I'm sorry, but why do you have to yell it?" I asked.

"Because it hurts. I'm on the outside, getting pummeled," Jay said.

Then I heard a grunt and a smack. I looked through the wall of nerds to see that Jay Parnell had been knocked unconscious and was lying on the gym floor. I hoped Mr. Muscalini would blow the whistle, but unfortunately, he did not. Unconsciousness was not a game ender. Neither was casual bleeding. I wasn't sure how he defined casual bleeding, but it seemed to be anything that didn't require a tourniquet or amputation.

Jay was not a heavy kid, but the rest of us were on the weaker side. His dead weight (not truly dead, just unconscious) pulled down Timmy Faulkner and Alex Chu, the three of them with arms locked. The weak link of the nerd herd had been exploited like the poorly-designed ventilation system of the Death Star in Star Wars.

"No!" I screamed, as fluorescent lighting surged into the gaps of the herd. Blinded by the light, I did not see the dodgeball leave one Randolph Warblemacher's hand. Despite the fact that I joke that his middle name is Nancy, he throws like a beast.

The dodgeball connected with my skull like a brick. I lost all functioning in my body. I may have tinkled a little bit and I could not hold myself back from saying, "I'm wearing yesterday's underwear. Inside out and upside down." I then collapsed to the ground.

I don't know how long I was out for, but I woke up to a whiff of chicken crotchatorie. The smell was like an atom bomb to my system. "Armageddon is here!" I yelled, popping up off the ground, ready to run to the nearest bomb shelter.

"What?" Mr. Muscalini said. "Why the heck did you say that?"

"It smells like the world just ended," I said, like he was a total idiot.

"Oh, yeah. I use this two-year old chicken crotchatorie instead of smelling salts. It works much better. The nerd revival rate is nearly 2x."

Ben chimed in nervously, "Revival? How many nerds have died playing dodgeball?"

Mr. Muscalini shrugged, seemingly not caring. "I don't know. I stopped counting. We haven't had any in a bunch of years," he said, almost disappointed.

"What? Are you serious?" I asked.

"I don't kid about dodgeball."

Randy peered over the huddle around me. "Warblemacher seven hundred. Davenfart zero." He cackled as he walked away.

3

———

We made it through the week. Only one nerd from my gym class got concussed from our final middle school dodgeball game, and it wasn't me. It was a win, as far as the nerds were concerned. Well, at least for all of us but the concussed Timmy Faulkner.

The class trip debacle also seemed to have died down. Calling Calvin and Channel 2 didn't have the desired effect. Once the news picked up the story, it was deemed fake news and sensationalist trash. I think it was the first time Calvin actually got a story even close to right. But whatever. We had bigger issues to deal with.

The carnival was starting. All the eighth graders were required to volunteer, which seemed a lot less like volunteering and more like indentured servitude, now that I think about it. Thankfully, my girlfriend, Sophie, was student class president and got us a good gig. I do think she could've done a better job of getting us a location a bit farther away from Mr. Muscalini and the petting zone for our less-than-esteemed and sociopathic mascot, Grimmwolf the Gopher, though.

Most kids didn't seem to know about Grimmwolf's demented demeanor and lined up in droves to pet the beast.

I watched from our lemonade stand, as Mr. Muscalini held Grimmwolf in his oversized hands and thrust him toward an unsuspecting child.

"Isn't he incredible?" Mr. Muscalini asked.

The small boy, who couldn't have been more than seven, ducked a savage attack meant for his jugular vein. The boy stepped back in fear.

"Oh, it's okay, little man. He won't bite," Mr. Muscalini said, as Grimmwolf snapped repeatedly at the boy.

The boy promptly ran away.

Mr. Muscalini placed Grimmolf on the table next to him. "You hungry, boy? Want a hamburger?"

Mr. Muscalini pushed a paper plate toward Grimmwolf. A tasty-looking burger patty sat alone in the middle of the plate. Grimmwolf glared at it.

"You want ketchup, don't you?" Mr. Muscalini's shoulders slumped. "Sauce calories count, too, Grimmwolf. You can't eat a lean piece of meat and then toss a whole bunch of sugar on top and think that's okay."

A ten-year-old girl stepped forward toward Grimmwolf, her hand outstretched toward pet the savage beast. Grimmwolf surged forward, his teeth clamping down on the poor girl's tiny fingers. She promptly burst into tears.

"Suck it up, girlie!" Mr. Muscalini said. "It's just a scratch." He looked at Grimmwolf and baby-talked to him, ignoring the girl, "Okay, you can have ketchup just this once, baby boy."

I walked over to her and took a look at her finger. "It's

okay. It's not bleeding. I've got some ice over here at the lemonade stand."

Sophie arrived and quickly bagged some ice. The girl was still crying, so I poured her a glass of lemonade, as Sophie placed the ice on her reddened finger.

"Does that feel better?" Sophie asked, softly.

I shook my head, as I watched Mr. Muscalini return with Grimmwolf and a burger doused in ketchup.

The little girl ran away after seeing her mother approaching.

"We got a great spot next to Grimmwolf," I said, shaking my head.

"I didn't make the floor plan," Sophie said. "But I got you a burger." She nodded to a cheeseburger loaded with lettuce, tomato, and my favorite combo of condiments: ketchup, mustard, and mayo.

"Thanks."

"And I did get us this gig selling lemonade," Sophie added.

"I may have to answer to Armpit Hair about that free glass of lemonade I just gave away," I said.

The annoying voice of one Randolph Nancy Warblemacher rang out behind us. "Abusing your presidency? Shocking." He was not shocked. "And how is our First Lady, Mr. Davenfart this morning?"

Sophie turned around. I could feel the heat of her anger in the air. "I have never once abused my presidency," Sophie said, outraged.

Randy ignored her. He looked down at our tip jar, which had a single dollar bill inside. He took the dollar out of the jar, straightened it out, and then put it back in. "Here's a tip for you," he said with his annoying smile. He looked over at Mr. Muscalini, then leaned in and whispered, "I'm going to ruin you both by the time we graduate. Or I graduate. I'm not going to deal with all your nonsense in high school. You're not gonna make it through the week."

"Is he saying he's going to kill us?" I asked Sophie.

"No," Randy scoffed. "Just get you expelled."

"Oh, okay. That's more up your alley," I said.

Sophie was not as understanding. "Are you joking? You think we're the problems here?"

"Yeah, it's quite obvious to anyone." Randy grabbed a lemonade and gulped it down.

"That'll be $50, Randolph," I said, holding my hand out.

He slapped my hand away. "Get out of here."

I said, "I was thinking the same thing."

We were interrupted by a little boy, who couldn't have been more than five or six years old. The boy tugged on Randy's shirt and said, "Excuse me, Mr. Warblemacher?"

Randy turned around. "What do you want, kid?"

The boy held up a pen and a piece of paper. "Can I have your autograph? I wanna grow up and play football just like you," the kid said, awe struck.

Randy smirked at me. "How many nerds want to be you, Davenfart?" He looked at the kid and said, "I know." Randy signed the paper and returned the pen.

The boy turned to walk away. Randy called after him, "Hey, kid. Believe in your dreams." So cliché.

"Nice speech," I said, mockingly. "I dreamt I punched you in the face. I think I'm gonna take your advice."

Randy's fake smile vanished. "Shut up, Davenfart. I knew you dreamt about me. So weird. And you don't have the guts to punch me."

Oh, how I longed to put Randy in the Camel Clutch and devastate every egotistical fiber of his being. But he was kinda right. Or very right, but I was not gonna give him the satisfaction. Sophie didn't have the same concerns that I did about punching Randy. She surged forward, led by her fists. I stepped in front of her to keep things from escalating. Randy wasn't the kind of kid who wouldn't hit girls. And while Sophie was tough, she could only take down Randy with a bow and arrow, as she did during the Renaissance Fair.

"That's not very presidential, Ms. Rodriguez, but then again. Shocking," he said, with no shock whatsoever.

"We should've put wheels on this stand. So we can wheel away from this clown," I said.

Randy walked away, still flapping his gums. "Always running away because you're not good enough. Not tough enough, Davenfart. You're a disgrace."

I shook my head as Randy walked away. I looked at Sophie, who was still staring at Randy, her chest heaving in fury.

"I need some comfort food," I said. I plopped down and started scarfing down my cheeseburger. I forgot about Randy as soon as the grilled burger and condiment combo ensnared my senses.

Ben walked past Randy, pointed at him, and said, "Look! A clown!"

Randy took a menacing stepped toward Ben, who promptly jumped back and nearly dropped his hotdog. Randy didn't respond to the clown comment. Instead, he smirked and asked, "Is that ketchup on your hotdog there, Gordon?"

"No, it's blood. I'm a vampire," he said, sarcastically.

"Enjoy," Randy said with a chuckle.

I pointed across the square to Randy's evil girlfriend and called out, "Oh, look. Regan's talking to Derek."

Randy's head jerked around so quickly, I thought it

might pop off. Pity that it didn't. He must have a very strong neck to support his oversized head and ego. He and my brother, Derek, were teammates and huge rivals for the school's athletic glory.

Randy said, "What the-" and then rushed off toward a group of athletes and cheerleaders.

I looked at Ben and asked, "Do you think something's wrong with your hotdog?"

"I don't know. He asked about the ketchup."

"I just had ketchup on my burger," I said, concerned.

"Definitely suspicious," Sophie said.

Ben said," I'm not eating it now." He tossed the plate onto the table. The hotdog bounced and then settled against one of the lemonade cups.

My buddy Luke snuck up behind us, as he often does. So much so that his nickname is Luke the Lurker. "I'll eat it!" he yelled, excitedly. Luke grabbed the hotdog and nearly downed half of it with one bite. "That's good," he mumbled, with half the bite hanging out of his mouth.

"You know what's less than good?" I asked. "Watching you eat that."

"Plus, it might be poisoned," Ben added, nonchalantly.

Luke shrugged and continued eating. "My dad said I eat so much junk my intestines are like a bomb shelter."

Speaking of eating junk, I looked around. "Where's Just Charles?" I was concerned. He did not handle situations like the carnival well. Lots of sugar and lack of parental supervision meant increased risk of an Evil Chuck sighting, his sugar-induced alter ego.

We didn't have a chance to figure it out, because mayhem broke out. Shocking. First, there was a commotion by the portapotties. Angry words being exchanged. Bodies jostling. Next, there were screams behind us and then people running and screaming while heading toward the growing commotion by the portapotties. It didn't take long to figure out what was going on with the ketchup. Even though spirit week hadn't even started, the spirit week pranks had begun. And Randy had seemingly struck first with a devastating blow.

Without warning, I took my own blow to my left eye, which I later figured out was Mr. Muscalini's elbow. I fell to the ground, as Sophie shrieked. Shaken, but still conscious, I watched Mr. Muscalini run through the crowd with Grimmwolf under his arm, leaving a disgusting trail of goop that was seemingly generated by Grimmwolf's butt. Mr. Muscalini knocked over at least a dozen grade schoolers like they were tiny bowling pins. Unfortunately, he was so intent on getting to the bathroom that he didn't appreciate the fact that he got a strike.

And then my stomach gurgled like nothing I had ever heard.

"What the heck was that?" Sophie asked.

"Was that an earthquake?" Ben asked, helping me to my feet.

"No," Sophie said. "I used to live in California. Definitely not an earthquake, but something funky is going on."

"Yeah, it's going on in my stomach," I said, looking down at it, my eyes wide in shock.

Sophie looked at me, concern in her eyes. "What is?"

"Mayhem," I said, and took off running.

I weaved through the crowd, holding my butt, for fear that it might explode. My mouth went dry and I started to feel dizzy. True, that happened most times I ran more than seven feet, but this was different. My vision was getting cloudy. Thankfully, I had Grimmwolf's trail to follow. I took it one step/squirt at a time.

I arrived at the portapotties to find none other than Max Mulvihill, my friend and bathroom attendant, in the middle of the chaos.

"Max! What's going on? I gotta get in there!" I yelled.

"We have a humanitarian crisis!" Max yelled back. He called out to the crowd, "If you have to do #1, you're gonna have to wait! If you have to do #2, line up on the left! If you have to do 1.5, line up on the right!"

"What the heck is 1.5?" somebody asked.

I was concentrating too hard on holding it in to answer his question and explain the merging of #1 and #2 into a disgusting and devastating combination.

In response to Max's announcement, nearly two thirds of the group lined up on the right, on the #1.5 line, myself included.

My stomach gurgled. "Ahhh, I think I have an alien in there!" I was pretty convinced that my butt was going to explode right there, which would cause two things to happen. Since I wasn't wearing a diaper (don't laugh- it wouldn't be the first time I did that in middle school), Sophie would immediately dump me (no pun intended), and I would be ridiculed for the rest of my life. Randy would surely name me 'Dumpy Drawers Davenfart.' or 'Diarrhea Davenfart.'

I called out, "Max! Speed this up!" If there was a silver lining in all of this, it was that whatever was in the ketchup had explosive properties, so the line was moving pretty fast. Still, I was running out of time. There was so much stomach rumbling going on, it sounded like Armageddon was on its way. In our pants.

Thankfully, I was next in line. I danced around, focusing all my energy on clenching my butt cheeks together like a bank vault door. Kenny Weick exited the portapotty in front of me with a smile. I surged past him, grateful that I had made it without losing my girlfriend or my dignity. It wasn't pretty, but neither would the back of my pants have been if I hadn't dealt with it. It was the first time I had ever said, "Ahhhh, farts!" with relief, and not condemnation or concern.

4

I shall never speak again of the episode that took place at the carnival. Well, at least the portapotty part. So, don't bother asking. Not sure why you would, but in the off chance you might, I wanted to make it clear.

I was at Frank's Pizza with Ben and Luke, gearing up for finals week. We chatted while we waited for a steaming, hot pie to be delivered to our table.

Ben shook his head and said, "I can't believe we made it. I didn't think we would. Do you remember our first day?"

I laughed. "Yeah, we almost gave up on all of sixth grade before we even sat down for lunch. I did get a fist full of beef stroganoff to the face from my wonderful butt-chinned brother, but I also met Zorch from that experience. And Sophie, of course, later that day."

Ben added, "We saved the dance that year."

"And the musical?" Luke added, unhelpfully.

"Ahh, who could forget Santukkah! The worst play ever written about Hanukkah and Christmas. Or any subject, for that matter," I said.

"And performed," Ben said.

"Speak for yourself," I scoffed. "I was awesome."

Luke quipped, "In your underwear."

"Wardrobe malfunction. Had nothing to do with my performance."

Ben said, "You mean like setting the place on fire?"

"Not helping, Benjamin. But you're not far off, I guess. The science fair was a disaster, too. But we did win Battle of the Bands that summer."

"You been following Goat Turd?" Luke asked.

"They're crushing it in Europe," I said.

Ben continued our reminiscing, "The class trips have been on the tougher side."

"Yep," I said. "I got my butt whipped in the Renaissance Fair, but Sophie took down Randy and Regan. And Butt Hair."

Luke said, "Rotten River?"

I shook my head. "Too soon, bro. Too soon."

Ben asked, "Cupid's Cutest Couple Contest?"

"Let's not go there, either. What else?"

"The Comic Con!" Luke said.

"We saved the world!" I threw my fist into the air. "Well, C.T. Walsh's career, anyway. I miss that guy."

"Such a handsome man," Ben said, out of nowhere.

"Meh," Luke said, shrugging.

I continued, "We had the election."

"Babybots," Ben said.

"Do not speak that name, ever," I said. "And now graduation."

Ben smiled. "After all that, it'll be nice to just cruise through finals and into the summer."

"Totally," I said.

But there would be no cruising. Did you really expect there to be?

Ben looked around and said with a crack in his voice, "I'm gonna miss this place."

Frank walked by. "What's the matter wit you? You eata spicy pepper?" Frank asked with an Italian accent.

"No, he's just a little sad to be moving on from middle school and leaving Frank's behind," I said.

"Everybody take a 'lil piece of Frank's when they leave."

Luke pointed to the lobby. "Can I have that picture of you and the President?"

"No," Frank said.

"Okay," Luke said, shrugging.

"I didn't mean take-a my stuff. I tell you what. You very special to me. I'm a gonna make-a you the besta pizza pie you ever gonna eata."

Ben seemed to cheer up a little, as Frank walked toward the kitchen.

"You're not dying, dude," Luke said. "We're just graduating to high school."

"You can still order pizza from here," I said.

"I know, but it's our joint. The high schoolers go to Harry's Hot Dog Den. That's just weird."

"I know," I said. "They're pretty good, though. I mean, who doesn't love a good hot dog?"

"I can't even think about ketchup right now," Ben said.

"Why do you put ketchup on your hotdog?" I asked. "That's your first mistake. Kids use ketchup. Men use mustard."

Ben looked at me and said, "Unsubscribe."

"Huh?"

"I'm unsubscribing from this conversation." Ben changed the subject. "Did you check out your finals schedules yet?"

Luke said, "Mine's a piece of cake. I have one a day for the week and then I'm done."

Ben asked, "How about you, Austin? You gotta ace them all."

"Mine's pretty tough," I said.

Ben pounded his fist on the table. "You gotta take down Randy. He can't win valedictorian."

"My schedule's crazy. I'll do the best I can. I have three finals on the same day and then two more the next day."

Luke asked, "I thought we couldn't have more than two in a day?"

"I have high school science. They don't care that it interferes."

"Bag it," Ben said. "You gotta win."

"But my science test goes on my college transcript," I said.

"Where can we hit Randy the hardest?" Ben asked.

"In his face? His crotch, maybe?" Luke asked.

"No, dude. I meant for finals," Ben said, with a face palm.

Luke smirked, "So sorry. I think we should hit him in the crotch anyway."

I laughed. "Have at it, man."

"I thought you were gonna do it. I'm not doin' it," Luke said.

I rubbed my non-butt chin and thought for a moment. "Randy's weakness is español. He hates it."

Ben nodded. "Well, then you need to crush him there."

"El squasho!" Luke said, slamming his palm down on the table.

"Sounds like somebody else needs some español help," I said, laughing.

≈

I SAT at the table in my basement with Sophie, going over Spanish test packets. I was pretty good at Spanish on my own. My mother is fluent, which helps, but Sophie was my secret weapon. It's her parents first language and she's fluent, too.

We were in the midst of a pretty serious study montage, which consisted of a variety of highs and lows, as all good montages do. I'm sure you've seen some good ones on TV or in movies. Ours went something like this.

Frustrated, I crumpled up my study guide and threw the paper across the room as hard as I could. I grabbed my shoulder in pain from the epic toss. I yelled, "Ahhh, farts" in Spanish. Of course, I missed the garbage.

Sophie and I studied from the crumpled-up study guide.

I paced around the basement, answering questions from Sophie. Her anger bubbled over and she used both hands to swipe our books from the table, which crashed to the floor and my pinkie toe. I hopped around on one foot, fighting back tears.

I iced my poor pinkie toe while sitting on the couch. Sophie tried to comfort me, but I ignored her, still angry at her ferocious attack against one of my favorite toes.

Sophie eased my pain by feeding me a piece of pizza. All was forgiven. We hugged. I hobbled back to the table to study.

We studied for the next few hours, then watched Spanish soap operas, which I am pretty much hooked on now. The drama is just so intense.

We both passed out on the table. I woke up with a pizza slice stuck to my forehead. Sophie had a half-eaten crust tangled in her curls. I never loved pizza crust so much in my life.

Sophie peppered me with more questions that I didn't know the answers to. I took comfort in eating the pizza that had been previously stuck to my forehead.

Sophie went through the questions again and I got them right! We ended with a hug as if I had just won the World Series or Super Bowl at the buzzer. Did the World Series or Super Bowl actually have a buzzer? I'm a nerd. I have no idea, but you get the point.

I looked at Sophie and said, "Estoy listo! I'm ready to crush Randy."

5

It was the last day of Advisory of my middle school career. Oh, the memories. Actually, I don't remember much of what went on in Advisory. Basically, ever. I missed half of them after being called down to the principal's office and the other half I was trying to catch up on sleep. Apparently, Ms. Armpit Hair was also feeling a little nostalgic.

The Speaker of Doom crackled. Mrs. Murphy's voice echoed with pity through our classroom, "Austin Davenport to the principal's office."

Nobody even looked at me. If a regular kid got called down to the main office to meet with the principal, there would be a lot of "ooohs" and "aaaahhhs" and a ton of questions. For me, it was so commonplace, it had become a non-event. I slipped out of my chair and nodded to Just Charles.

"Adíos, muchacho!" I said, with a salute. I was so ready for the Spanish final.

I walked down to the main office and entered the bustling headquarters of Cherry Avenue Middle School.

Mrs. Murphy gave me a sympathetic look and said, "Good morning, Austin. You know the drill."

Before I could even sit down in the waiting area, Ms. Pierre opened her door and motioned for me to enter The Armpit, her hairy, smelly lair.

I plopped into the uncomfortable chair across from Ms. Armpit Hair. She stared at me for a moment, sizing me up. I twiddled my thumbs while I waited for her to tell me the ridiculous reason I had been summoned down to her office.

"Well, Missssster Davenport. You seem to have taken the cake this time."

I threw my hands up. "I did not steal a cake. This is ridiculous!"

"No, it's an expression."

"Oh, well, I like cake, so if it's just sitting around, I might take a little unauthorized nibble, but I haven't seen any cake around here."

She did not look enthused. "Let's speak in terms of hot dogs and hamburgers."

"I'm fluent in both of those languages. Y español," I said.

"Bless you."

"I didn't sneeze," I said, shaking my head.

"Mr. Gifford ran some tests on the condiments. Do you know we came up with?" Ms. Pierre asked me, accusatorially.

"Ummm, the mayo was expired because our cafeteria is the worst?"

"No. Well, yes, but that's not the point. The ketchup had high doses of Sennosides."

"How much?" I asked, not even knowing what Sennosides were.

"I was hoping you would know. It was enough to nearly destroy the poor small intestine of our fine mascot," Ms.

Pierre said, faking concern. "He's on life support and the doctors need more information."

"Grimmwolf has the intestines of an ox," I said. "He'll outlive the Apocalypse."

Ms. Pierre looked like she might hurl, which happened often during her conversations with me and even when speaking about me, as evidenced by the valedictorian announcement. She shook her head and said, "This is disgusting. Let's never discuss that rodent's intestines again."

"I can't make any promises," I said. "You never know when gopher intestines might come up in normal conversation."

Ms. Pierre ignored my comment and pointed her finger at me. "Did you or did you not spike the ketchup with laxatives?"

"I *ate* the ketchup and nearly blew up my own small intestine. I had nothing to do with it. You should talk to Randy."

"That's what a guilty person would say."

"How many guilty people claim they almost blew up their own small intestine?" I asked, defensively.

"I meant accusing another student," Ms. Pierre said.

"Ask Max if I did it," I said.

"Who is Max?"

"Never mind." I didn't want to alert Ms. Armpit Hair to the presence of Max Mulvihill. Given her greediness, she would probably want a cut of his revenue. And if Max found out it was me, I'd have to pay to pee again, and I wanted no part of that.

Ms. Armpit Hair said, "What evidence do you have that you ate the ketchup?"

"Ask Sophie. She got it for me. She witnessed it."

"Hardly an unbiased witness," Ms. Pierre retorted.

"Ask Kenny Weick. He was in the portapotty right before me."

"A somewhat-intelligent guilty person would pretend to have the same affliction as everyone else. How do I know you ate the ketchup?"

"Check the portapotty," I said. "I don't have any evidence."

She nearly retched up breakfast.

I shrugged. "Sorry, you asked. What evidence do you have that I spiked the ketchup?"

"Go back to class," Ms. Pierre said, waving me away.

I WAS on the verge of finals week. I sat in the den with Leighton and Derek, reading over a study guide.

My mother walked into the room and said, "Are you ready for your Spanish exam?"

"Sí, señora," I said, with a smile.

"I forgot to make a donation for spirit week and the carnival fundraiser. Take this." My mother handed me a folded-up bill.

"What are you giving money to the school for? The whole thing's a sham."

"I thought you liked school?" she asked, cocking her head to the side.

"I *do* like school. I was talking about Ms. Pierre's fundraisers. I'm pretty sure she buys new shoes with that."

"Oh, Austin. You're such a kidder," she said, and then left the room.

"Whatever," I said.

I looked back at my study guide and tossed it aside. I decided to do a final study brush up for Spanish. Well, it wasn't really studying, per se. It was more like practicing my insults. There were only a few times I was confident enough to insult my brother to his face. When I had laryngitis. When he had his headphones on blast. Or when I was speaking Spanish.

Derek looked at me. I smiled and said, "Tu eras un sacapuntas."

My sister leaned over to me with a smile and whispered, "Did you just call him a pencil sharpener?"

Derek shrugged and said, "Muy taco," which meant 'very taco.' It appeared as if he needed his own study montage.

Derek put on his headphones and flipped on his iPad.

I looked at Leighton and said, "Yes, it sounds like a bad insult though, doesn't it?" I looked at Derek and said, "Tienes un trasero gigante en tu cara". It basically meant he had a giant butt face.

Derek called out, "Mom! Austin said something about my butt in Spanish."

Figures those are the only words he understands in Spanish.

"Austin, what did you say?" my mother asked from the other room.

Aaahhhh, pedos.

I sat in Spanish class, waiting for Señora Fuentes to hand out our final exam. I knew there wouldn't be anything about pencil sharpeners or butt chins, but I felt prepared, nonetheless.

Señora Fuentes placed the test on my desk, smiled, and said, "Buena suerte, Austin. Try to write about something other than tacos this time."

"I make no promises," I said, smiling. I do my best writing about tacos, burritos, and nachos. Fajitas, too. I pulled the paper toward me and got down to negocio or business.

I ended up writing a fabulous essay on multiculturalism. It was basically about how cuisines other than Mexican should utilize the tortilla more. There was a bunch of other nonimportant stuff like verb conjugations and pluralization. Just a bunch of -ations. Nothing to be concerned about. I crushed it all. Had I not studied a lot with Sophie, it would've been hard, but I felt confident. I took a few glances over at Randy during the test. Stress clearly littered his normally-unpleasant, but flawless face.

I finished early and watched with pleasure as Randy wrote furiously. His normally perfectly-coiffed hair was strewn about, sticking up in all directions, a product of, well, too much hair product and stress.

Señora Fuentes said, "Lapices abajo," or pencils down.

She walked over to Randy and said, "Lapices abajo." Randy kept writing. She tugged at the paper while Randy held it firm. "Señor Warblemacher. Pencils down!" She pulled the paper from his grip. I smiled. Typically, I don't relish other people's misfortune, but Randy is not most people. I'm not sure he's even a person. I think he might be some sort of soul-sucking vampire. That would answer a lot of open questions.

As we left the room, I made it a point to slip into the line right behind Randy. Normally, I'd try to stay as far away from him as possible, but I just couldn't help myself after witnessing his near-meltdown.

I peeked my head in-between him and Jayden. I said, "If I didn't know that soulless didn't sweat, I'd say I thought I saw perspiration percolating on your forehead at the end of the exam."

"Shut up, Davenfart," Randy spat.

He didn't follow with any retorts, which was not typical. I'd gotten under his skin. I didn't know how to proceed. In the past, even when I had him beaten big time, his arrogance wouldn't let him admit any frustration.

"So, that's a yes?" I asked. "I'm now questioning everything I know about science. Do Undead creatures sweat or does Randy Warblemacher actually have a soul?"

"Keep talking, Davenfart, and the only science project you'll ever be involved in is your own autopsy."

"Can you say that into my phone after I hit record?" I asked. "I love your hair, by the way."

Randy just shook his head. He walked away, but then stopped at the glass window by the stairwell, fixing his hair. It was back to perfect in no time. I was disappointed I hadn't taken a picture. But it would forever be burned in my mind, so I got over it quickly.

"Toodles!" I called after him. I watched him with a smile on my face. Unusual, I know.

6

The next morning, I was stressed. It was the morning of my three-exam day. I had high school science, history, and then math. It was going to be an intense day. There was a lot riding on it. I knew Randy would ace his own science and math exams. While my own science exam didn't count for valedictorian, it counted on my transcript, which was important for college.

And Randy's confidence was back. With a vengeance. After I took my high school science exam, which was a battle of the wits between Ms. Kelvin and I, I was already drained. I could only imagine how poorly Flea felt, who was not nearly as good as sciencing as I was. You may remember when he blew off my beautiful eyebrows.

Anyway, after a tough exam, I was certainly not in the mood to deal with Randy. I saw him in the hallway at Cherry Avenue as I was waiting for Sophie to be finished with her science final. He walked out of the classroom, his smirk leading the way. He poked me in the shoulder with his index finger while he walked by.

"I just aced the science final, Davenfart. I'm gonna be valedictorian and there ain't nothin' you can do about it."

"Well, you might fail English with that grammar, but so what? I take high school science. I don't have time for middle school science."

I looked over to see Mr. Gifford, staring at me, while clutching his chest. "That hurts me to my core."

Randy walked away without another word. It was getting strange.

Mr. Gifford stepped toward me, breaking out into a huge smile, "But in other news, my love life is spectacular! You really did it this time, Austin. I knew there was a reason you were my love guru."

"Really?" I assumed he was referring to our disastrous class trip, during which I inadvertently smacked Mrs. Funderbunk in the face with my paddle while rafting down Rotten River. It set off a series of fortunate events for Mr. Gifford's love life, proving himself worthy to the picky Mrs. Funderbunk, his forever love, or at least since last year.

Mr. Gifford beamed. "We're going to summer in France together while she works on her new musical."

"Oh, God," I mistakenly said out loud.

"What's wrong?" Mr. Gifford asked.

"Nothing. Just nervous about my finals." I didn't have the heart to tell him that his girlfriend was the worst playwright in the history of Broadway or even way, way, way off Broadway. She had written our sixth-grade holiday musical, a mashup of Christmas and Hanukkah, called Santukkah! It had resulted in me baring my Batman underwear to the entire crowd. Randy also puked in the baby manger (which he wholeheartedly deserved and a highlight of the night for me) after I lit the stage on fire. The entire auditorium was drenched. Not with puke. The sprinkler system went off from the fire. Some of that wasn't Mrs. Funderbunk's fault, but I'm sticking by my story.

Mr. Gifford continued, "I'm sure you'll do fine." He leaned in and whispered, "I'm hoping you win valedictorian."

"Thanks."

Mr. Gifford patted my shoulder and said to Sophie, "You got a smarty pants, here. Even though he's wearing shorts." Mr. Gifford then broke out into uncontrollable laughter.

I forced a few laughs. "Good one," I said, not wanting to dampen his spirit. He'd been through so much in his love life, a lot of it was own fault, no doubt, but still. He was happy and I didn't want to take that from him.

Sophie and I walked together to our history final.

Randy walked in just after us. It was as if I hadn't just shut him up two minutes earlier. "Hey, Davenfart. I'm gonna crush you so hard it'll go down in the history books. Being valedictorian is like manifest destiny."

And he thought I was the dork. Using history terms in his insults. It was pathetic.

"You think you being valedictorian is destined by God? I knew you were arrogant, but this is unbelievable, even for you."

"It's inevitable, Davenfart."

I decided to use his historic insults (they weren't good enough to be written into the history books- I just meant they were about history) against him and see if I could throw him off his game. "Dude, I'm gonna crush you like the Battle of Bull Run. The Union got control of the Mississippi River and the rest, well, is history." I said that, knowing full well that it was not the Battle of Bull Run that turned over control of the Mississippi to the Union, but the Siege of Vicksburg. It was a stone cold move in nerd circles.

"I'm gonna bull run right over your face," Randy said, heading over to his seat across the room.

I looked at Sophie and gave her a wry smile. "We'll see about that," I whispered.

Dr. Dinkledorf gave out the exams. It was 50/50 between multiple choice and essays. There were two questions on Manifest Destiny, which I'm sure Randy got right, but there was an essay on both battles of Bull Run. I hoped Randy made a mistake.

After the exam, I passed by Dr. Dinkledorf's desk.

He looked at me expectantly. "How are you feeling about the exam?" He leaned in and whispered, "I'd really like to see my prized student win valedictorian."

"I feel pretty good," I said, excitedly.

And then I remembered my mother's donation. "Did you hand in the money for the fundraiser?"

"No. I have it here in my desk."

"Good. My mother wants to make a donation," I said, handing Dr. D. the money.

"Wonderful. She's too kind. But I would expect nothing less from the mother of a boy like you."

"Thanks," I said, embarrassed. I guess he was too old to remember that she was also the mother of Derek, The Butt-Chinned Bandit.

Dr. Dinkledorf opened his desk drawer, pulled out a small lock box, and flipped it open. Cash nearly flew out, it was filled so high.

"Too bad that's going to buy our school another statue of Ms. Armpit Hair," I said.

"Let's hope she's had her fill," Dr. Dinkledorf said, disapprovingly. "Well, glad you think you did well on the exam. Fingers crossed for valedictorian," he whispered.

Little did I know that exam would lead to my ultimate doom, even though I aced it.

I MADE it through my three-exam day, but was staring down a doozy. Most kids might think having one gym exam would be an easy day. Those kids weren't me. I feared whatever Mr. Muscalini was going to cook up for us. And he very well could cook us up something with a lot of protein. You never knew with him. We might be eating beef liver or even bugs or chugging protein shakes until we puked. Although after he had a bug on our class trip and nearly puked, I'm pretty certain he'll think twice before incorporating bug eating into the curriculum.

Not to mention, there could be rope climbing, dodgeball, or just about any sport, none of which I was good at. I wasn't sure how many points I'd get if I hid in the Nerd Herd to avoid getting slammed with a dodgeball. While effective, it was frowned upon by the purists.

I waited for class to start with Ben.

Ben said, "I'm worried he's going to have a dodgeball machine that is gonna hurl balls at us at ninety miles an hour."

"Yeah, but if you get knocked out, at least you get to go to the nurse. Nurse Nova is sick and tired of all the head injuries around here. She'll let you stay the whole period. I'm worried about a Burpee Bonanza. There's no getting out of that."

Ben said, "Burpees. I mean, I like the name, but they sound a lot more fun than they are."

"Preach, brother," I said.

Mr. Muscalini entered the gym as if he was attending a funeral. My first thought was that Grimmwolf had eaten through his metal cage and either escaped or died.

"Gather 'round," he said, glumly.

"What's wrong, sir?" Randy asked, like the kiss-up that he is.

Mr. Muscalini shook his head. "I just got off the phone with the Chairman of the Athletic Department. New regulations dictate that your final must be a written examination, since we didn't give any written tests the entire year. Something about being inclusive with nerds who can't play sports."

The Nerd Herd broke out into cheers and hugs.

Ben yelled, "My life has meaning again."

Alex Chu broke out into tears. Jay Parnell did the sign of the cross and raised pray hands to the sky.

Normally, Mr. Muscalini would make us run laps for an

outburst like that, but he was too distraught to care. I looked over at Randy. He was seething and so were the rest of the jocks.

We sat in the bleachers and took a multiple-choice test. It was a piece of cake. I was coasting into valedictorian. Randy was gonna get crushed.

As I walked out with Ben, he asked, "What did you put down for the question about how to dodge a dodgeball?"

"The answer was simple. Get out of the way."

"Dang it. I put 'form nerd herd.' Did he really think we'd say to put on Harry Potter's invisibility cloak? I can't believe that choice was on there."

We laughed it off.

Ben said, "I don't care that I got it wrong. My dad will be so proud that I got a ninety-something on a gym test."

It didn't take Randy long to shake off his disappointment about the phys ed final. He smirked and said, "Well, lookey what we have here. The king of the nerds."

"At least I'm king," I said.

"Not for long."

I was tired of the banter. I was gonna try to take a different track. "Please tell me we're not gonna do this all through high school."

"You have a better idea?" Randy said, laughing.

"Yeah, we ignore each other. My life would be complete. Your silence completes me."

"Awww, so sweet," Ditzy Dayna said, walking by.

"She's so dumb," Randy said.

I smiled and said, "That's the first thing you've ever said that I've agreed with. Well, except that one time you said you were stupid."

"I never said, 'I'm stupid'!" Randy yelled.

I suppressed a laugh. "You just did."

It probably wasn't the best course of action, because Randy doubled down. "I'm going to make your life miserable in high school." Randy thought for a moment. "Yeah, that feels right. I try to let the universe guide me. You wouldn't understand."

"I thought you were gonna get me expelled?" I asked.

"Oh, right. I forgot. Thanks for the reminder!" Randy said, enthusiastically.

"This has been incredibly riveting and spiritually uplifting, but I have to pee," I said.

Randy shook his head. "So, juvenile, Davenfart. I hope you grow up over the summer. Then you'll have the maturity of an eight-year old."

"Adiós, Randolph," I said, with a salute.

I turned around when Randy said, "Hey, Davefart, I would tank the English final if I was you."

I huffed. I couldn't believe there was a chance he could beat me for valedictorian. I corrected him, "If you *were* me."

"That's what I said."

"No, you said '*was*'."

"Whatever, Davenport."

"Not whatever, Randolph. The subjunctive mood is not whatever. God, I can't believe you're the second smartest kid in the school."

"*You're* the second smartest kid in school." Randy got up in my face and said through gritted teeth, "Tank English or take a punch to your face. I wonder if it would look better after that."

Ahhhh, farts. But maybe not. Maybe he could dent my chin and my parents would finally love me and my new butt chin. Nah. Ahhh, farts is probably the better thought. The butt chin wouldn't last, but the emotional scars of their ultimate rejection would.

7

I stood with Ben and Sophie after all our exams were done. I nibbled on my nails as we discussed a plan.

"What do I do?" I asked. "I don't want him to bust my beautiful nose."

Sophie said, "I love your nose. You should tell someone."

I furrowed my brow, "Tell someone that you love my nose? Do I have to? Ben's here. He heard it."

Sophie rolled her eyes.

"Oh," I said. "Tell somebody that he wants to punch me. Everybody already knows that."

"Yeah, but this is different. He's threatening you."

"I don't want to be that kid. I can handle it," I said, not sure if I really could. My brother had beaten me up enough throughout my life, I knew I'd survive. But he was smart enough not to break my nose.

"But you shouldn't have to. You can't always win," Sophie said.

Ben said, "We're nerds. We prove that every day."

Sophie's shoulders slumped. "That's not what I meant. You guys are emotionally draining sometimes."

"Oh, God. There's Calvin," I said.

"Go tell Calvin about Randy," Ben said. "He'd love the drama."

Cheryl hurried over to us. I nodded to Calvin. "What's with him?"

"Oh, that hack? Calvin is doing a 'Through the Years' piece on our class with a big interview with Ms. Armpit Hair."

"Of course, she'll take the spotlight," I said.

I looked the other way as we passed by Calvin. I heard him say, "Anybody know who that kid was who got put in the Camel Clutch at the science fair two years ago?"

It was me, but I wasn't about to tell him. It was embarrassing enough at the time. I didn't need to relive it. Or the glitter bomb that blasted me in the face. I sometimes still wake up haunted by glittered unicorns. I don't recommend it.

And then the Speaker of Doom echoed through the hallways. "Austin Davenport, Sophie Rodriguez to the main office. Austin Davenport, Sophie Rodriguez to the main office."

Sophie looked at me, her eyes wide. It was a highly unlikely Speaker of Doom demand. Typically, I got called down during Advisory or it was announced in the classroom.

"Is somebody dead?" I asked.

"Who could be dead that they needed us both?" Sophie asked.

"Good point. Maybe they think we killed Randy," I said, scratching my head.

And then I saw Randy and realized he was not, in fact, dead. Unless his ghost was there to haunt me for all eternity, which sounded like something he would do.

"Whatever it is, it can't be good," Sophie said.

"Let's go, I guess." I'd never not gone down to the office when called. I wondered if I could just get away with it, but then came to my senses. Of course, I couldn't. Ms. Armpit Hair would show up in my living room. Without using the front door. Or perhaps any doors. I would just look up from the TV and she would be there, staring at me, holding a detention slip. Or maybe a Chinese throwing star would slice right through my burrito, cutting it in half., spewing hot sauce into my eye and blinding me for life.

Sophie and I headed to the main office. I moped down the hall, racking my brain about what I could've possibly done wrong or been accused of this time. I fantasized about getting sent off to LaSalle Military Academy, so at least the punishments would be doled out evenly. Everybody there was treated like garbage. That seemed pretty fair at the time. I wondered if Ms. Armpit Hair had some sort of Wheel of Detention that she spun every day that would tell her the made-up reason she was going to use that day for my punishment.

I opened the door to the main office and let Sophie in first. Mrs. Murphy looked at me, a concerned look on her face. "Have a seat," she said, nodding to my personal lounge, also known as the waiting area.

I did as I was told. I know, shocking. Sophie slipped into the seat next to me.

"Are you getting used to this yet?" I asked.

"Never," she said, annoyed.

"I'm numb to it. Pinch me."

Sophie pinched me.

"Owww!" I said.

Sophie laughed.

I shrugged.

Sophie looked at Mrs. Murphy and asked, "What's this all about?"

"Don't know, I'm afraid," she said.

I said, "I'm pretty certain it's about the unfairness of life. Is it not enough to have the only noncontoured chin in a family of big butt-chinned kin? I have to endure this? Whatever it is?"

Sophie nodded, but didn't say anything.

Ms. Armpit Hair emerged from her office, her upper lip quivering. She didn't say anything. She didn't have to. Her face said it all. Her anger was off the charts, but I had no idea why. Perhaps because I existed. Perhaps because the sun came up another day. Perhaps the Wheel of Detention broke. So many possibilities.

Ms. Armpit Hair pointed to us with two fingers and then down at her feet. I don't know what it is about the two-fingered point, but it is much more emotionally-rattling than the single finger point. Sophie and I both stood up quickly and hurried into Ms. Armpit Hair's office.

"Close the door," Ms. Armpit Hair said through gritted teeth.

I looked back at Mrs. Murphy with the hopes that she would be ready to intervene in case our lives were threatened. She looked back at me, sympathetically, but didn't seem to have 9-1-1 on speed dial.

"Sitown," Ms. Pierre yelled, the words blurring together. I had never seen her lose her cool before.

"What's wrong?" Sophie asked.

"Wouldn't you like to know?" Ms. Armpit Hair spat.

"Ummm, yes. That's why I asked," Sophie said, quietly.

It didn't help the situation. I was just glad it wasn't me adding fuel to the fire. But then Ms. Pierre's words hit us like a ton of bricks.

"There's money missing from the recent carnival fundraiser," Ms. Pierre said, studying our faces like she was a human lie detector. I was pretty surprised we weren't actually hooked up to a real lie detector.

"That's terrible," I muttered. "Why are *we* here?"

"You're here to give it back," Ms. Pierre said.

Sophie nearly exploded. "You think we took the money?"

Ms. Armpit Hair said, "I don't think anything. Eyewitness testimony *says* you did."

"That's ridiculous," I said.

"I don't believe this," Sophie said. "I would never take money from the school."

Ms. Armpit Hair didn't consider our defense. She continued as if we didn't say anything, staring directly at me. "You, I'm not surprised, but you, Ms. Rodriguez, I thought you were going inspire Austin to turn his back on his devious ways. It appears as if he's had a negative influence on you."

I leaned forward in my uncomfortable chair and said, "I didn't-"

But she cut me off. "There will be a full investigation. And I can't promise you, Ms. Rodriguez, that there won't be an impeachment trial as it relates to your position as eighth-grade class president."

Ms. Armpit Hair might've hurt Sophie less had she reached into Sophie's chest, torn out her beautiful, beating heart, and fed it Grimmwolf the Gopher, who most certainly would've torn it apart with his razor-sharp teeth and demonic soul.

Sophie's face morphed white. She gripped both armrests on her chair. Not out of anger, which was usually her first negative emotion. It was seemingly to steady herself out of shock. Or keep her from vomiting on her shoes.

Before either of us could say anything, Ms. Armpit Hair said, "That is all. May God have mercy on your souls."

I felt like that was a bit much, but I was not about to say anything to dig ourselves deeper into a hole. I stood up and said, "Come on, Soph. Let's go."

Sophie nodded, not saying anything. I helped her up and ushered her out the door. We were supposed to go to lunch, but I wondered if I should take Sophie straight to the nurse. God knows the cafeteria's nutrition wasn't going to settle her stomach.

Thankfully, we had a little more leeway during finals, so instead of the cafeteria's chicken a la cringe, we had lunch at Frank's instead. We sat with our crew, dumbfounded by the turn of events.

And it got worse. Cheryl entered with a handful of papers and slammed them down on the empty table.

"You're not gonna believe what the Gazette is printing in the summer edition tomorrow," Cheryl said, seething.

Sophie muttered, "My obituary?"

"Pretty much," Cheryl said, clearly not sensing the mood of the crew. She slid into the seat next to Just Charles. "Let me read you the draft." Cheryl read from the papers, "President ruined. Davenport to blame. Impeachment imminent! Eight-grade embarrassment and soon-to-be ex-president, Sophie Rodriguez, is facing substantial backlash amid an investigation into missing funds."

"I can't get impeached. I've done nothing wrong!"

"We need a plan," Ben said. "What do we do?"

Luke thought for a moment and said, "I think we go for the Supreme. How can you pass up meatballs, sausage, and pepperoni on one slice?"

Sophie glared at Luke.

"I think Ben was talking about the missing money, not the pizza order," Sammie said, most likely saving Luke's life.

"Oh, right. I do my best work after being well fed. Sorry."

Sophie said, "It's clear. We're finished. I'm going to be impeached. We're going to be expelled. There's nothing we can do. They're just going to lie and cheat until they win."

"It's the Warblemacher way," I said, defeated.

"There's always something we can do," Cheryl said.

Ben looked at me and said, "Austin, you're one of our best idea generators. What are you thinking?"

One of the best? The best. Ben's slight, whether intended

or not, kick-started my brain into action. "I've got a plan," I said.

Sammie smiled and said, "I knew you would. What is it?"

"Order a Supreme. Enjoy our last morsels of Frank's Pizza and then fake our deaths, hire a coyote to sneak us into Mexico, and open a taco stand in Guadalajara."

Ben said, "I hate to be a downer, but what makes you think you can run a successful taco stand in Mexico?" Like that was the only limiting factor of our plan.

"I've lived through like 650 taco Tuesdays. I've picked up a trick or two. Use quality ingredients and overcharge for the guacamole. It's a no brainer," I scoffed.

"That sounds pretty good actually," Luke asked. "Would you use pico de gallo?"

I shrugged. "I think it would be an optional condiment. I think if you give the people a choice, they'll choose you."

Sophie asked, annoyed, "Can we talk about the real issue here?"

Luke said, "Is nothing sacred? We're talking about tacos! You don't just interrupt a taco convo."

Sophie's eyes narrowed.

Luke said, "Perhaps we went a little too far. Let's wrap this conversation up for another time." He looked at Ben. "Just a little burrito joke that I thought was apt."

I looked at Sophie. Her face suggested that was not apt. Not apt at all.

I forced myself to focus on the solution and not the problem. I said, "We all know it was Randy."

"Or Dr. D. just misplaced the money," Cheryl said.

"If that was the case, don't you think he would've paid it back? Why would there be eyewitnesses turning us in?" I asked.

I said, "We need to talk to Dr. D. I'll call him from Mexico."

"Not funny, Austin," Sophie said, cracking a smile for the first time since we learned of the allegations.

"How do we prove Randy did this?" Cheryl asked.

If only that question could be answered with overpriced guacamole.

I WENT BACK to school after Frank's. I cornered Dr. Dinkledorf in the hallway. It wasn't hard. He had no reason to avoid me, plus he moved like a turtle. A really old turtle.

"Excuse me, Dr. Dinkledorf?" I said.

He beat me to the punch, no pun intended. "Austin, I expedited the grading for yours and Randy's final exams. You did very well. I can't believe Randy thought the Union took the Mississippi during the Battle of Bull Run," Dr. Dinkledorf said, shaking his head.

"He did? I knew he would!" I yelled, forgetting about the bigger issue at hand.

"That's a pretty strange thing to cheer about," Dr. Dinkledorf said. "We shouldn't celebrate other people's lack of knowledge about Bull Run."

"Of course," I said. "I just want to win valedictorian so badly. I need every point I can get."

"Ooooh," Dr. Dinkledorf said. "I might have to go through his essay again, see what these old eyes may have missed." He gave me a wink and a smile.

And then I remembered the bigger issue.

"I was actually looking for you. I was hoping you could tell me more about the missing funds and why you think I was implicated along with Sophie."

Dr. Dinkledorf's brow furrowed, "Oh, right. I forgot about that. I don't know much. Here's what I do know. I didn't report it. Ms. Armpi...er Pierre said there was an anonymous tip. Then I checked the money and it was missing."

"It wasn't me. I promise."

"Austin, my boy. Do you think that I don't know that? You're one of my most trusted students."

I nodded thoughtfully. "Then someone is trying to take us down. To sway the valedictorian race. To take down a presidency." I knew that last bit would get him, being the history teacher and knowing his love for democracy. "We must save the Republic!" I added for effect.

"Save the Republic!" Dr. Dinkledorf yelled, thrusting his fist in the air. He looked at me and asked, "How do we do that?"

I shrugged. "I was hoping you would know."

"Nope. Not a clue."

Aaaahhh, farts.

8

The next morning, I sat at the kitchen table with Derek, both of us eating oatmeal, as my mother moved about doing odds and ends. I stared out the window, mesmerized by the tick-tick-tick of the sprinkler system, numb to my current state of affairs. That is, before my mother rushed to the garbage pail, gripped it with two hands, and let out a toe-curling, "Hwuullllaaaah!"

I looked over at my mother and without thinking, said, "That's appetizing."

"Yeah, gross, Mom," Derek said, dropping his spoon on the table.

My mother looked up at us, spit dripping from her mouth. She wiped it with the sleeve of her robe. "So sorry," she said, seemingly not sorry at all. "I'm growing a baby in my stomach. What have you done today?"

"I, ummm, wiped my butt," I said. "I also microwaved this. Forty seven seconds of perfection." I nodded at my oatmeal, again not thinking.

My mother stood up and stared at us. "Oh, yeah. Those are similar in skill."

"Sorry, Mom. I'm a little out of sorts."

She took a deep breath. "Join the club. I'm sorry, too. I didn't mean to be rude. This has just been a really tough one. The worst one by far."

"Who was the toughest before?" I asked, knowing full well it wasn't me.

My mother didn't hesitate. "Derek. Definitely."

Derek chimed in, "That's because I'm tough." He flexed his bicep like Mr. Muscalini would've done.

"Whatever," I said.

"No, you're just a pain in the butt," my mother joked. I laughed until Derek made it clear it wasn't funny by giving me a death stare. My mom changed the subject, "What's going on at school today?"

Derek shrugged. "Stuff."

"Oh, stuff. Thank you for that insightful answer. Such depth," my mother said, laughing.

My brother was not known for his emotional or personal depth, excluding the depth of his butt chin.

My mother continued, "What about you, Austin?"

I smirked. "Oh, not much. Sophie's got an impeachment hearing."

"What?" my mother shrieked.

"Someone's trying to take down the great nation and Republic of Cherry Avenue Middle School."

"Sounds like Randy's doing," Derek said, in between bites of his oatmeal.

"Most certainly," I said. "With a little help from Ms. Armpit Hair."

My mother sighed. "Austin..."

"What? She likes it," I said.

Derek laughed. Yeah, I dare you to call her that to her face."

"Oh, I will," I said, confidently. Through double-paned soundproof glass. Although with her espionage skills, I'm pretty certain she would read my lips and slice off my ear with a ninja star, all without breaking the glass.

THAT MORNING at school was a joy. The Speaker of Doom crackled to life. Ms. Armpit Hair kicked off the morning announcements with an electric, "Good morning, Gophers!" I'd learned that with Ms. Armpit Hair, and her predecessor, Principal Butt Hair, there was a 1:1 correlation between their excitement level and the student's gloom and doom. She continued with enthusiasm, "I want to address a serious situation and share with you that we will hold an impeachment hearing for our *current* eighth-grade student president, Sophie Rodriguez, this afternoon. All student government officers are required to attend. And it is suggested that all students participate as well. Have a spectacular daaa-aaaay!"

Just Charles looked at me with anger. "Did she win the stinkin' lottery, or something? I've never heard her sing during the morning announcements. I mean, she's not Mrs. Funderbunk."

"She just wants to humiliate us in front of the entire school," I said. Which Mrs. Funderbunk also does every time we put on a school play, but at least she's not trying to embarrass us on purpose.

SOPHIE SAT ALONE at an eight-foot table, center stage in the school auditorium, fidgeting with her hands. Ms. Armpit Hair sat in the center of a similar table that stood perpendicular to Sophie. Dr. Dinkledorf was to her left while Rose Dumbleton, the class secretary, was to her right. There was another table across from Ms. Pierre, seating four other officers from the school's government. As far as votes were concerned, I was pretty certain Dr. D. was on our side, but he was canceled out by Ms. Armpit Hair, and Rose was probably against Sophie as well. Which meant that we needed three out of those four other officers to vote against impeachment.

I sat in the front row of the auditorium, which had a few students scattered around. Most of the kids there appeared to have missed the bus and just wandered in, looking for something to do rather than actually caring about the impeachment hearing. Our eighth-grade class was not one for democracy. It was something I was grateful for at that moment, but concerned about for the long term.

Randy was there, of course, with his sidekick, Nick, who was gobbling up popcorn.

"You want some?" Nick asked.

Randy waved them away and said, "I don't eat empty calories."

Ms. Armpit Hair stood up, straightened her dashingly brown pants suit, and began her diatribe, "Impeachment. You've all heard this serious word. Very serious," she said, as if she was talking about death. "Impeachment is the process of bringing charges against an officer of the government for crimes."

Dr. Dinkledorf interrupted, "Alleged crimes. There has been nothing proven against Ms. Rodriguez."

"Yes. Yes." Ms. Armpit Hair rolled her eyes. "If we agree to move forward, there will be a trial which will determine if Ms. Rodriguez will be removed from office."

Dr. Dinkledorf interjected again. "This is a serious process. I urge you to take great care."

"If you are familiar with the Grand Jury process," Ms. Pierre said, as all of our eyes glazed over in boredom, "this is not a trial. It is just to determine if there is enough evidence to proceed with a trial that would remove Ms. Rodriguez from office."

"Our Secretary, Rose Dumbleton, will lead this impeachment hearing. Rose?"

Rose was as snooty as they come. She stood up and smirked at Sophie, as if she was waiting for this moment for her entire life. Rose took out a sealed envelope and opened it.

Rose said, "I have eyewitness testimony that I will read

to you. This person has given a sworn statement and asked to remain unnamed until it is completely necessary."

"Randy," I whispered to myself.

Rose read the letter, "I saw Austin Davenport sneak into Dr. Dinkledorf's classroom while it was unattended. Given Austin's penchant for devious deeds, I followed him. He opened Dr. Dinkledorf's top drawer, removed the lock box, and then removed money. Later, I saw him give Sophie Rodriguez that same money. I also overheard them discussing spending that money on a date. Why someone would want to date Austin Davenport? I don't know."

I thought that last part was not a necessary detail, but there was nothing I could do about it.

Rose smiled, as she tucked the letter away. She looked at Sophie and said, "Ms. Rodriguez, do you have any evidence to refute this eyewitness testimony?"

"How do I prove that something didn't happen? This person is lying. I didn't take any money. Neither did Austin."

"So, you have no evidence proving your innocence?" Rose chuckled.

"Do you have any evidence proving that *you* didn't steal the money, *Ms. Dumbleton?*" Sophie asked.

"This is not my impeachment hearing," Rose said, smirking.

"What happened to innocent until proven guilty?" I called out.

Ms. Armpit Hair said, "Again, this is not a trial. The same standards don't apply to this type of hearing." She looked at me, beaming. I wanted to puke.

Ms. Armpit Hair stood up, grabbed a small ballot box and said, "Now that you've heard the significant evidence from the eyewitness, and the lack of evidence from the alleged criminal, please place your impeachment ballot in this box."

Dr. Dinkledorf stood up. "With all due respect, Ms. Pierre, that is your opinion. I move to strike this entire proceeding, due to your biased nature."

"Overruled," Ms. Pierre said, narrowing her eyes at Dr. Dinkledorf.

Nobody knew what to do.

Dr. Dinkledorf didn't seem to know, either, but he stood up and yelled, "I overrule you! As the history chairman, I am the leader of the student government program."

"As the principal of this school, I am the leader of the history chair. I would recommend that if you would like to continue to operate in that role, you should sit down in *your* chair. Now."

Dr. Dinkledorf took a deep breath and sat down.

Ms. Pierre walked around to each of the government members, collecting folded up pieces of paper that would either exonerate or doom my lovely girlfriend. When she was finished, Ms. Pierre sat back down in her seat, dumped out the box in front of her and Dr. Dinkledorf and said, "Count them, Mr. Chairman."

I wanted to slap her smirky face, but I was afraid she would take me out with a Chinese throwing star just for thinking it. Could she read my mind? It was a possibility.

Dr. Dinkledorf ignored her smirk and began to count the votes. Sophie took a deep breath and fidgeted with her hands.

"One vote for impeachment. One vote against. One vote for. One vote against. One vote against."

I closed my eyes, hoping for a miracle. It was 3-2 in favor of Sophie. We just needed one of the final two votes.

"One vote for impeachment," Dr. Dinkledorf said, seemingly disappointed.

I opened my eyes, willing a vote against impeachment.

Dr. Dinkledorf opened the paper slowly. He stared at it for a moment. I tried to read his facial expression, but he was so old and wrinkly, it was really hard to make sense of any of it. And then he read the final vote, "One vote *for* impeachment."

I hung my head in my hands, trying not to cry. I was so tired of this nonsense. I was used to taking it myself. It hurt more to see it happening to Sophie.

I looked up to see Sophie wiping tears away. She stood up and walked off the stage. Dr. Dinkledorf followed her quietly. Ms. Pierre seemed happier than she'd ever been while she spoke with Rose, who most definitely voted against Sophie.

"Revenge," was all I could say in my deepest, raspiest

voice, as I stood up and followed Sophie out of the auditorium. Randy gave me a thumbs up as I left.

I tried to focus. I tried to think of something good to say, knowing that Sophie was going to be a mess when I found her. I hustled out of the auditorium and found Sophie sitting under a dogwood tree in the Atrium. I sat down next to her.

"It's not the end," I said, rubbing Sophie's shoulder. "This doesn't mean anything."

"Of course, it does," Sophie said, angrily through tears. She stood up and stormed off without another word. I watched her go, knowing it was not going to be helpful to her or our relationship if I followed.

9

After that joyous occasion, I decided to swing by the boys' locker room to clean out my gym locker. That way, I wouldn't have to bring home my smelly gym clothes on the regular bus and risk peer ridicule. Not that anybody else's was any better. But the day already stunk, so I figured it couldn't get any worse. I was wrong.

I stopped outside the doorway. I thought twice about entering, but decided to go along with the original plan. The stench hit me like a punch to my olfactory system. The stench was *so* bad. I think I lost time.

I opened my eyes and looked around. I found myself leaning up against the wall, holding the door open for somewhat fresh air. Adolescent sweat and nerd fear hung in the air like a dense fog. "What year is it?" I whispered to myself. How long had I been out for? Based on the smell, there was stuff in the locker room that had been decomposing for years.

I should've probably just left the clothes behind, but I worried about Zorch's health (if he was still alive), having to deal with all the odiferous clothes left behind. Maybe that's why the guy had lost his sense of smell and actually enjoyed Ms. Geller's cafeteria food. That, or they remove trainees' olfactory systems during custodial training.

I heard the door open behind me. I thought it was just another brave soul whose mother wanted to know why his gym clothes hadn't been home and washed since the previous summer. I didn't think much about it, as I popped open my locker.

And then I heard the voice of a possible ghost in Randy Warblemacher, "What a surprise meeting you here, Davenfart."

"Oh, is it? I'm sure you followed me in here." Or in death, you apparated. I knew he hadn't apparated here as a living soul. That would've meant he knew magic. And he was not Harry Potter. He was the worst sort of Muggle you could possibly imagine.

"Did not."

I just shook my head. "What's your point?"

"Since we're here, just having randomly bumped into each other, I think we should have a little chat."

I rolled my eyes. "I thought we were."

"Shut your mouth when we're talking. Honestly, Daven-fart. You're so rude sometimes."

I was so confused. "How am I supposed to shut my mouth when we're talking? I'm not a ventriloquist. But it's pretty obvious that I'll be the valedictorian."

"Whatever," he said.

I decided to just walk away. I turned away from Randy and closed my locker. He grabbed me by the shoulder and turned me toward him with some force.

Before I knew what hit me, Randy, well, hit me. With a blow to my stomach that knocked all the air that I'd ever inhaled out of my lungs. I gasped for breath, as I doubled over.

Randy leaned down and whispered, "I'm going to win valedictorian."

I stood up and mustered enough breath to say, "I don't see how, when you're second best." Despite the fact that I was claiming to be the smartest kid in the school, it was a dumb thing to say, evidenced by the second punch I received in the same spot. I nearly threw up my breakfast. From last week.

I coughed and then spit. I aimed for Randy's overpriced sneakers, but missed. Apparently, nerds can't even spit with accuracy. How is that fair?

The door opened again. I wanted to call for help, but didn't have the lung capacity to do it. The familiar whistling of my favorite custodian, Zorch, echoed throughout the mostly-empty locker room.

Randy whispered again, "Watch out. Next time, it'll be worse."

I wasn't sure how it could be worse unless he was

somehow able to defy human limits and punch a hole right through my stomach and come out the other side.

Randy slipped around the back of the lockers, away from the oncoming whistle.

Zorch did a double take and then headed toward me. "Austin? Are you okay?"

I nodded. "I think so. My spleen definitely popped, but I'm pretty certain spleens are optional organs."

"What's a spleen?" Zorch asked.

"Exactly. I'm just glad I didn't get a swirly."

"We haven't had a swirly in years. Bullies are not as menacing as they used to be, I guess." Zorch shrugged. He slapped me on the back.

I winced. "You're telling this to the kid whose spleen just got popped."

Zorch nodded. "Right. It's a conversation for another time. I see that now." He put his hand on my shoulder. "Do you need to go to the nurse's office?"

"I don't want to give Randy the satisfaction. I'd rather just die so he'll have to live with it for the rest of his life."

"I know you're the genius, but that doesn't sound like the best plan you've ever had."

10

I bumped into Dr. Dinkledorf on the way out of school. He was wheeling his creaky, old suitcase of history books behind him. Unless it was his joints that were creaking? I wasn't sure. Dr. Dinkledorf was a modern marvel. He was so old, nobody was sure how or why he was still alive. Anyway, he smiled when he saw me.

"Austin, my boy! How goes it?"

I shrugged. "I've been better," I said.

Dr. Dinkledorf stopped on a dime. True, it wasn't that difficult given how slow he was moving, but don't let that distract you from the concern that showed on his face.

"What's wrong?" he asked.

"Randy beat me up in the locker room," I said, adding a groan for good measure.

"He did what?"

"He punched me in the stomach twice. And told me he was gonna win valedictorian."

"Does he want you to just let him win? By threat of force?" Dr. Dinkledorf said, astonished.

"It was a little more than threat of force. It was actual fist force."

Dr. Dinkledorf grabbed my shoulder and said, "We have to report this. Take him down for good. We will not be intimidated!"

Easy for him to say. I was pretty intimidated.

"Let's go meet with Ms. Pierre. She's still here. I just left the office."

"Yeah, great," I said, sarcastically. It was quite likely she would punch me in the face to add to my wounds.

"This is preposterous," Dr. Dinkledorf said, leading me back into the school.

I was glad he was on my side, but in all fairness to me, he wasn't the one getting his spleen popped. I wasn't sure he even had a spleen. He was so old, I wondered if it had already disintegrated. I'm a science geek and all, but I had never actually studied the spleen, much to my chagrin at that moment.

As we walked, I asked, "Sir, what do you know about spleens?"

"Bless you," he said.

"No, the organ. The spleen."

"Do people even have those anymore?" Dr. Dinkledorf stroked his beard in thought, as we continued making our way to the main office, or what I've decided to affectionately call The Temple of Doom. He continued, "I've always wanted a gizzard though. It's a pity that humans don't have them."

I nodded. "Hmm, deep scientific thoughts for a history teacher."

"We've been through a lot, me and you," Dr. Dinkledorf said.

I nodded. "Thank you for always being there for me."

"It has been my pleasure to serve," Dr. Dinkledorf said with a bow. He grabbed his back as he straightened up. "Ugh, my lumbar!"

"That's not a real thing, is it?" I asked.

We arrived at The Temple of Doom. Dr. Dinkledorf opened the door and held it for me. I wasn't sure if he was just being polite or wanted to make sure I wasn't going to leave him behind. It was always better to have witnesses. I entered to find only Mrs. Murphy behind her desk. Normally, there was a bustling of activity.

Mrs. Murphy furrowed her brow. "Can I help you, Dr. Dinkledorf?"

"Yes, Mary. We need to see Ms. Pierre."

She nodded and pointed to the waiting area. "Have a seat."

Ms. Pierre stuck her head out of her office. "What's next on my schedule, Mrs. Murphy?"

"Dr. Dinkledorf and Austin are here waiting to see you."

"Anything more important than that?" she asked, apparently not caring that we were living beings with feelings.

"No, I'm afraid that's it."

I looked at Mrs. Murphy, who shrugged back.

Ms. Armpit Hair said, "Very well. Follow me, Misterrrr Davenport."

I did as I was told. I slumped into my usual seat. It was a bit hard. Without thinking, I asked, "Can we get more comfortable chairs in here?" I looked at Dr. Dinkledorf and asked, "What do you think?"

"Wars have been started for less," he said, squirming in his chair and seemingly failing to find a comfortable position.

She looked at me like she was going to kill me, which I wouldn't put past her. I was pretty certain she was a Navy Seal or FBI agent. At least I had a witness. True, he was really old and she could take him out too and just blame it on his old age or maybe his faulty gizzard, but still.

I backtracked a little. "It doesn't have to be a memory foam recliner or anything, but a thin cushion wouldn't hurt."

"The boy does have a point," Dr. D. said with a grunt.

"We don't have the budget for that."

I looked at her giant throne. I was pretty certain it had both heating and cooling units attached, as well as massage capabilities. It also might've been able to go airborne. There were strange jet engine-looking things attached to the back of the chair (I know, my sciencing is off the charts.)

Maybe it was a missile launcher? If Sophie made it through the impeachment trial unscathed, Ms. Armpit Hair might take down the whole place with the push of a button. I feared for humanity should our cafeteria explode. Not only was there the potential for physical damage, as over-cooked chicken nuggets rained down upon unsuspecting citizens like the tasteless bricks that they are, but the radiation blast would be off the charts. Some secret government agency would have to come in with hazmat suits and quarantine the place. Only Grimmwolf the Gopher would survive.

Ms. Armpit Hair continued, "And do you think I want you to be comfortable sitting in the principal's office? I think you're comfortable enough flouting authority. You're a flouterer. Why are you here? What is it that you want?"

"I prefer to be called a floutist," I said.

"Why are you here?" Ms. Pierre asked again, annoyed.

"Oh, my bad. I want to report an assault. Randy Warblemacher punched me in the stomach. Twice," I said, with a groan.

Ms. Pierre asked, "Did you deserve it?"

"No student deserves to be punched in the stomach," Dr. Dinkledorf said, outraged.

She didn't appear to agree. "Were there any witnesses to this alleged assault?"

"Mr. Zorch was there," I said.

"He saw Randy strike you?"

"Well, no. He came in after."

Ms. Armpit Hair suppressed a smile. "So, there were no witnesses?"

"Well, no. I have evidence, though."

"Did you capture it on video?" Ms. Armpit Hair asked, concerned.

"No. I captured it on my stomach," I said. I lifted my shirt to show the still-red mark on my gut. The one that most certainly popped my spleen. "That looks exactly like Randy's fist. It's a spitting image."

And then belly button lint fell out of, you guessed it, my belly button, and landed on her desk. It was quite a large amount, given the small size of my belly button. She looked at it. I looked at it. Dr. Dinkledorf looked at it. I didn't know what to do. It was obvious that it was there and she was not happy about it. I tried to make it fun, so I picked it up and shot it at the waste paper basket.

"Davenport from long distance!" I let the lint fly. Of course, it missed. I shrugged. "Oops."

Ms. Pierre took a deep sigh and looked up at the ceiling. After a moment, she said, "Very difficult to punish a student for something like this without witnesses. It's a real pity. I'm sure you can understand."

"That's not fair," Dr. Dinkledorf said.

"But I witnessed it," I said, annoyed.

"Dr. Dinkledorf, do you think I can punish every student who has an accusation made against them without evidence? In your studies of history, have you ever come across a society that has thrived under such actions?"

Dr. Dinkledorf shook his head like he had just been parented. "No, I guess not."

I was ready to explode. "How can you impeach Sophie with some random eye witness named Randy Warblemacher, but not do anything when my eyes saw him punch me in the stomach? And I don't even want to get into what happened to my spleen."

"It's an interesting conundrum," Ms. Pierre said, thoughtfully. "Sometimes the rules aren't fair."

"I've been saying that for three years. Plus, you make the rules," I said, annoyed.

Ms. Pierre shrugged. "Be that as it may, there's not a whole lot I can do."

"Couldn't you at least talk to the boy and see what happened?" Dr. Dinkledorf asked.

"I could," Ms. Pierre said, nodding, but we all seemed to know that she would do nothing of the sort.

"Unbelievable," Dr. Dinkledorf said.

Ms. Pierre ignored him. And then her face lit up. "I have something for you, though."

She opened her drawer. I gulped. I was pretty certain that was her Chinese throwing star drawer.

But thankfully, she removed a note pad and began writing on it. She tore the paper off the pad and said, "Here you go."

"What's that?" Dr. Dinkledorf asked.

It's a detention slip for being late."

"Oh, I've always wanted one," I said.

Dr. Dinkledorf looked like his head might explode. "But school is over!"

"Okay." Ms. Pierre looked at me. "If you prefer, you have detention for throwing trash in the principal's office."

"What? I'm getting detention for belly button lint! This is ridiculous. Even Butt Hair wouldn't give me detention for that."

"*Butt Hair*? This is how you speak of your leaders?" Ms. Pierre scoffed.

Leaders was a strong word, but I did make a mistake in having said it.

"Let's make it a double detention, shall we? You can spend some bonding time with Mr. Braverman, your old detention buddy. I think he misses you."

"This is wholly unfair," Dr. Dinkledorf said.

"Would you like to join him, Dr. Dinkledorf?"

I wasn't sure she could give a teacher detention.

"You can't give me detention. It's in our contract."

"Are you sure?" Ms. Pierre asked, like she knew something we didn't.

Dr. Dinkledorf scratched his head. "No, actually. I'll have to talk to the union."

"You do that," Ms. Pierre said, angrily.

11

D r. Dinkledorf followed me out of the Arm Pit. Mrs. Murphy caught my eye as I walked out.

"Everything okay?" she whispered.

I shook my head. "Umm, no. I can't wait to get the heck out of this place. She's so unfair. And she's stealing from the school. Everybody knows it," I said, angrily. "Just look at her chair. I think she stole that from the U.S. Department of Defense!"

Once we made it out to the hallway without getting any Chinese throwing stars to the butt, Dr. Dinkledorf asked, "Is that how it always is?" It was a common question when I had a principal's office partner, or P.O.P.

"Pretty much. That was probably one of the better encounters, actually. Plus, I just made the Guinness Book of World Records for being the first kid ever to get detention for belly button lint."

"Good point. You will forever be in the annals of history. Perhaps my successor will teach it one day," Dr. Dinkledorf said.

"Your successor?"

"You think I'm going to teach forever?"

"Well, I did think you were a descendant of the Jedi Master, Yoda, who lived until 900."

Dr. D. laughed. "If only I had the Jedi Master's powers. I would defeat the darkness that rules over Cherry Avenue. Or at least keep me out of detention."

I MET up with Ben and Just Charles in the Atrium and told them the Randy story.

"How are you going to get payback?" Ben asked.

Just Charles didn't hesitate. "Fire ants in his underwear. Billy Plunkett did that to me in third grade after I pushed him down the slide. It was checkmate."

"Yes!" I said with a fist pump, then grabbed my spleen with a grimace.

"Where do we get fire ants?" Ben asked.

"I don't know. A fire ant farm?" Just Charles said.

"Google it," I said.

Ben bit his lip. "Do you think maybe that's a little too low, even for Randy?"

Just Charles said, "Yeah, I wouldn't wish that on anybody. Billy Plunkett didn't really know what he was doing."

Ben asked, "Do you still have the robo dialer from the Cupid's Cutest Couple contest?"

"Yes," I said, not sure where he was going with it.

"We could program it to call Randy over and over and over again," Ben said.

"I like it, but we need something more," I said. It's not often that I think about what Derek would do with the thought of following his lead, but I was desperate for payback. And then it hit me. "Derek would light a giant bag of poo on Randy's lawn."

"Randy would hate to stomp that out," Ben said.

"He wouldn't do it," Just Charles said.

"Charles is right. It has to be bigger than that. We need to dump a ginormous pile of poo right on his front lawn," I said.

"Where are we gonna get enough poo to do that?" Ben asked.

I smiled. "Horse stables."

"How are you going to transport the poo?" Just Charles asked. "A catapult?"

"A catapoooolt," I said, laughing.

"Good one," Ben said.

"Maybe we can have it delivered. The Cherry Hill Horse Farm isn't too far," Just Charles said.

I thought for a moment then said, "Yeah, but Mr. Matheson loves football. There's no way he'll drop that much poo on Randy's lawn."

"Will any adult actually do that?" Ben asked.

Just Charles shook his head. "Probably not."

I grabbed my chin in thought. "What about the Bisons?"

"You think the whole Bear Creek football team will just poop on his lawn?" Ben asked.

"No. Well, maybe. They hate our football team. Surely, they have a horse farm," I said.

Just Charles said, "Bear Creek doesn't even have a Starbucks."

"Well, we can try," I said.

"When's your mom getting here?" Ben asked.

"A few minutes," I said. "That reminds me. I gotta go get some stuff out of my locker." I just hoped Randy wouldn't be there to punch me in the stomach again. Given that the hallways were wide open, I figured I was in the clear.

I was mostly wrong.

Ben followed me to my locker after Just Charles got picked up. I grabbed my lock and entered the combo.

"Remember when you got Power Locked on the first day of middle school?"

"Yeah, it was awesome," I said, sarcastically. "Although, it set us up with Zorch. Without him, we would've had a lot more detentions and never would've saved the Halloween Dance."

"I didn't think it was possible for you to get more detention," Ben said, laughing. He cut his laughter short and asked, "What's that disgusting smell? It smells like low tide or worse, the cafeteria."

I opened my locker, the door slamming open with some sort of disgusting gop of goo pouring out onto me and the floor. It wasn't Grimmwolf butt goop, but it was pretty bad. Rotten fish to the face.

I spit out the fish guts in my mouth, sighed, and then looked at Ben. "That smell would be fish guts."

A bunch of kids walking by, laughed.

Randy arrived, pointed at me, and laughed. "Seafood....Surpriiiise!"

He high-fived Nick DeRozan and continued on down the hall.

"I'll look up the fire ants," Ben said.

"How about smirk-sucking leeches?" I said, wiping fish from my face with my fishy sleeve.

"That would be nice," Ben said.

"I'd better go get hosed off by Zorch. There's no way my mother is letting me in the car like this. She'll puke for the rest of the day, even without the morning sickness from her pregnancy."

"Later," Ben said, retching as he ran away.

I walked down the hallway, my head held high. I nodded to Mary Hart and gave a thumbs up to Jonathan Leo. Both ran into nearby classrooms and puked into the garbage pails.

The puke might've actually improved the smell. It was difficult to say being that my body was on the verge of destruction. I had a popped spleen, aching abs, and a torched olfactory system.

I made it to Zorch's Lair without making anyone else puke, which was a small victory.

I knocked and waited for Zorch to open the door. He looked at me with a furrowed brow.

I said, "The first day we met, you asked me if I wanted you to hose me down. I thought it was weird, but I now need those services."

"It certainly looks like it," Zorch said, leading the way back to the water spigot.

"How do I smell?" I asked.

Zorch smiled. "You kind of smell like the seafood surprise. So spectacular. It's one of my favorite meals that the Mrs. makes. Unfortunately, she doesn't cook that much at home. She gets tired of it after cooking all day. She puts so much energy into it."

I furrowed my brow. "What, like plutonium?"

Zorch turned around quickly. "She puts a lot of love into that food, Austin," he said, defensively. "Do you have anything against industrial-grade engine cleaner?"

I took a step back, shocked. "To eat?" I wasn't sure if Mrs. Zorch was putting that in the beef broth. It would make a lot of sense.

"To clean you up. You know my affinity for soaps and cleaners. The more stringent, the better."

Had it not been for Zorch's affinity for soap, I might never have saved the Halloween Dance back in sixth grade, turning it into the best foam party in the history of foam parties. That wouldn't ever make it into the history books, but it should. True, it had been the only foam party I had ever attended, but I checked with Dr. Dinkledorf, and he agreed, and he has a PHD in history. I think he wrote his dissertation on the history of foam parties and other soapy social gatherings.

"Is the cleaner okay for delicate skin? I'm not all calloused like the Neanderthal football players."

"Not sure. We'll just try it anyway," Zorch said.

"Yeah, I don't think that is such a great idea. How about I just get hosed off and put on my Black Plague-infected gym clothes?"

"I guess," Zorch said with a shrug, obviously disappointed.

12

My mother made me walk home while she trailed me in the car for two miles. She was adamant that she would puke, crash, and then kill all of us, including my impending butt-chinned sister currently residing in my mother's stomach. As if I need to add to my stench with adolescent sweat. Yes, I was walking, but that's still strenuous for a nerd, and it was hot out.

I took two showers and a bubble bath with lavender and a few of my other favorite essential oils. Surprisingly, dead fish trumps lavender, so despite my best efforts, I still smelled like the local fish market. After the power goes out.

It was so bad, even Barn Door didn't sit next to me on the bus to the high school the next morning. I was done with my science final, so I didn't even need to be there, but I needed to see Max. If there was anyone who could help me remove the stank that followed me around like a dark, smelly cloud, it was Max.

I waited for everyone to get off the bus before I headed out. I found it best to travel solo, as I avoided the stink eye (no pun intended) from my better-smelling peers. If there was any good news, it occurred during my interaction with Principal Buthaire. You must be thinking, come again? But I kid you not.

The Prince of Butt Hair spotted me from across the entrance. His first instinct was reach for his jacket pocket, which held his detention pad. He smiled wryly, as we locked eyes. He hurried over to me, barely able to contain his excitement.

"I thought I was done giving you detention for the year, Missssster Davenport. This is a lovely surp-" Once Principal Buthaire got within six feet of me, my stench hit him like a brick to the face. He threw up his hands in an attempt to shield the odiferous air from his being, but he could not. He tried to swat the stench away, but it seemed to only intensify his disgust.

"Ugh!" He grabbed his nose, turned and ran, and said in an even-greater nasally and whiny tone than normal, "We will meet again, Missssster Davenport!"

I pumped my fist. "Butt Hair repellent!" I finally figured out how to evade Principal Buthaire and his repugnant regime.

Unfortunately, I quickly realized that it would also repel my girlfriend, so I was pretty much back to square one. Or perhaps square negative one, as I would rather attract Sophie than repel Butt Hair.

I made it to Max's Comfort Station without issue, more desperate than I'd ever been. Even that first time when I almost peed in my pants. Max hovered over a table, trimming leaves from a beautiful bonsai tree.

"Whoa, Aus! You really got into it this time," Max said, covering his mouth and nose, as if about to vomit. He used his other hand to shield the bonsai tree.

"And this is after two showers, a bath with essential oils, and a hose down from Zorch. I should've gone with industrial-grade cleaner," I said, pounding my fist into my hand.

"Zorch loves his cleaners, doesn't he?"

I nodded. "Do you have anything that can help?"

"Of course. All organic. This is patent pending. My lawyer's working on it," Max said.

"Is he here?" I asked, curiously. One time when we were talking about patents, his lawyer popped out of one of the bathroom stalls. You never knew what you were gonna get with Max.

"Michael? Oh, no. He's in Dubai, working on an energy deal for me."

"I don't know how you do it. Come to think of it, how *do* you do it? Now that you've moved out of Cherry Avenue, can you tell me how you made all this happen?"

Max smiled and then said, "Mindset. Creativity. Online MBA courses."

"That's not what I meant. How did you run a private bathroom in a public school?"

"Those are trade secrets, bro. Maybe I'll tell you when you graduate high school. Maybe."

"Okay," I said. "It was worth a try."

"Now, back to the issue at hand." Max walked over and opened a cabinet. He examined a variety of bottles and containers.

"What's with the tree?" I asked.

"It's not just any tree. It's a bonsai tree. It's part of my Feng Shui."

"Bless you," I said.

"No," Max said, laughing. "Feng Shui. Chinese geomancy."

"Oh, that explains it."

Max grabbed a bottle from the bottom of the cabinet. "It originated in ancient China. It uses energy forces to harmonize individuals with their surrounding environment."

"Aren't bonsai trees Japanese?" I asked, confused.

"Very good, Aus. Japan is more known for bonsai, but it

actually originated in China, as well. The samurai used the caring of bonsai as a balance to war."

"Interesting," I said, not having any idea when I would ever need to know or use any of that.

"I took the best of the East and combined them. Feng Shui for the environment. Bonsai for the mind and soul. Now, before you kill all the energy in this room with that fish smell, let's get you taken care of."

"Thanks," I said, sheepishly.

BEN, Just Charles, and Luke were over my house. We were down in the basement. They forced me to sit across the room on a beanbag chair for fear of the smell, while they occupied the couch.

"Dudes, I need another slice of pizza," I said.

"Stay there. We'll throw it," Ben said.

"Isn't this getting a little ridiculous? Max got rid of the fish smell," I said, annoyed.

Just Charles grabbed a slice and held it like a frisbee.

"We can't take that risk," Luke said.

"Unreal. First of all, you can't throw and I can't catch. Why would we waste a perfectly good piece of pizza?" I asked.

Just Charles' shoulders slumped. He held his nose with one hand, took a huge breath and held it, and delivered a floppy slice of pizza with the other. He plopped the pizza onto my plate and scurried away. He released his breath and sat down.

"Ridiculous," I muttered.

"Let's get to the point of this meeting. Randy. We need to strike back. Strike back hard," Ben said.

"Like the Empire," I said, referring to Star Wars.

"What would Darth Vader do if he was in middle school?"

"Something with poop," Luke said.

"He'd make it fly across the room with his mind and blast Randy," Just Charles said.

"The poop war is about to begin," I said, in my deepest, darkest voice.

fter I woke up the next morning, I walked out of my bedroom and noticed Derek in the bathroom with the door open, his face nearly touching the mirror above the sink.

I needed info from him to strike back at Randy. "Hey, Derek?" I asked.

"I'm busy," Derek said, monotone.

"You're combing your non-existent mustache," I said, laughing.

He looked at me like he was about to slice me open with said comb. "My mustache needs to be cared for. Are you aware of the bamboo tree?"

"No, I'm more into bonsai trees. For the mind."

"The bamboo tree sets its roots for four years before it grows above ground. In that fifth year, it could grow a few feet in a day," Derek said, like he had just given me the solution to world hunger and bringing peace on earth.

"What's your point?" I asked.

Derek rolled his eyes. "What do you want?"

"What's the football captain's name from Bear Creek?" I asked.

"Bryce Lawson," Derek said, seemingly holding back puke. "I hate that guy."

"I couldn't tell. Bryce the Bison?" I asked.

Derek said, "Sounds like a mascot, not a captain, right? Why?"

"I thought I saw him at Franks. Maybe not."

Derek threw his mustache comb down. "They're encroaching on our territory?" he yelled. "I'd better not see him again or I might light a flaming bag of poo on his lawn."

"When are you going to outgrow that stage?"

"Did Superman outgrow flying? Did Wonder Woman just one day decide to toss aside her lasso of truth?"

"You're Wonder Woman?" I asked, confused.

"Shut up, Austin."

"So, let me get this straight. You're saying that lighting poop on fire is your super power?"

Little did he know that I was going to try to convince Bryce to deliver and the light the largest poo fire ever known to man right in the middle of Randy's front lawn.

I was heading into the middle school and nearly vomited. I wasn't pregnant nor did I have any rotten seafood dumped on me. It was the sight of Principal Butt Hair that made me ill.

"Misterrrr Davenport. Always a displeasure," he said, heading toward me. "I hear you are on the verge of expellation. Not surprised. I knew it from the first day I saw you."

"What? I am? What are you talking about?" I had forgotten about it, my eyes set on a pile of poo.

"You stole from the school," he said, simply.

"I did not!"

"Don't use that tone with me, boy. Or we'll start next year off with detention. If you're even going to be here."

Principal Butt Hair walked off, whistling like the happiest guy in the world.

I was stunned. I zombie-walked over to a bench in the Atrium, and fell into it. I hadn't thought about the seriousness of what Randy had accused us of. I know it sounds stupid, but Ms. Pierre was so focused on the impeachment, I didn't think about what would happen after. But for once, Principal Buthaire was right. If they could frame us for stealing from the school, we could get expelled, and maybe even sent away to some sort of home for juvenile delinquents.

Cheryl walked by and did a double take. "Austin, what's the matter?"

"I had an entanglement with Butt Hair," I said to Cheryl.

"I don't need to know about your problems with personal hygiene," Cheryl said, disgusted.

I shook my head. "No. I meant I had a run in with Principal Buthaire. He told me I was on the verge of getting expelled. I haven't seen him that happy in a while. If it wasn't at my potential demise, I might've been happy for him. The guy is so miserable all the time."

"I still can't believe they might expel you and Sophie," Cheryl said, shocked.

"Has the Gazette heard anything new?" I asked, concerned.

"No, but they keep anti-Austin and Sophie stories under tight wraps from me. They know where my loyalties lie. I'll see what I can uncover."

"Thanks," I said, but didn't feel any better.

And the day was just getting started.

"What's up, Davenfart?" Kyle Cerrone said with a chuckle, as he passed by. His cluster of Tennis Turds, as they were affectionately known, laughed along with him.

I furrowed my brow, as Kyle walked past. Only Randy's inner circle called me Davenfart. And the uppity Tennis Turds were far from friends with the brute football squad. I never had any issues with the tennis kids. They were a little snooty at times and they often wore white shorts after Labor Day, a significant social faux pas, but they kind of kept to themselves. They didn't normally go on the offensive. They were athletes, but it was tennis. It was low on the tough-guy totem pole.

Sophie ran over to me, a huge smile on her face. I shifted my attention away from butt hair, farts, and turds, and focused on my girlfriend.

"Hey, what's going on? What are you so happy about?" I asked.

"I just picked up my yearbook. I want you to be the first to sign it." Sophie unzipped her backpack and pulled out the yearbook. It was, of course, adorned with our less-than-lovable mascot, Grimmwolf the Gopher. Sophie flipped open the yearbook to my page and handed it to me, slipping next to me on the bench. I didn't want to ruin her spirit with the news from Butt Hair.

I checked out my picture to make sure all was okay. Not bad. It was a solid picture. No butt chin, but I could always draw one in at a later date. And then my heart dropped. I read the name underneath my picture and it read, you guessed it, Austin Davenfart!

Anger bubbled up inside me with ferocity. "Aaaahhhh, Davenfarts!"

"What's wrong?" Sophie asked.

"Randy," was all I could muster as an answer. I handed her the yearbook.

Sophie took the yearbook out of my hands and inspected it. "That Son of a Slytherin!"

I was still angry, but also quite proud at Sophie's Harry Potter insult. It was on. I mean, it was already on, but at that moment, it was really on.

I WAS with Just Charles and Luke at the Bear Creek Mall. Supposedly, Bryce Lawson worked there at the sporting goods store that his parents owned. I had no idea if that was true or what his schedule was, but we decided to check it out.

We entered into the sports superstore. Every bone in my body started to quiver.

Just Charles was apparently feeling it, too. "This doesn't feel right. We're nerds. We're not supposed to be here," he said, his voice shaking.

"We just have to push through it," I said.

"It's against our nature," Luke said.

"It's just a store. Fight it," I said, walking into the store in slow motion as if some sort of invisible force pressed against my effort.

A few people looked at us like we were crazy. An arrogant-looking high school kid who worked there looked at his older, bearded co-worker and chuckled. "Look. Nerds."

The older man seemingly had a little more empathy for our situation. He looked at us and said, "The lawn darts are in the back corner. Don't worry. You can make it."

"Back corner?" I asked. "Why would you do that to us?"

Just Charles brought me back to reality. "We're not even here for the lawn darts."

"Oh, yeah," I said. I looked at the older man. "Can you tell us where Bryce Lawson is?"

He furrowed his brow. "Sure."

The pompous kid said, "He's in the dodgeball section."

"The dodgeball section! They have those here?" I asked, in fear.

Just Charles dropped to his knees and cried out, "Bear Creek is Hell on Earth!"

The kid laughed. The older man rolled his eyes. "Knock it off, Charlie." He looked at us and said, "He's just messing with you. He's in the women's sports bra section."

That just might be worse. "Where's that?" I asked, my voice shaking.

He pointed a few sections over.

"Thank you," I said, steeling my nerves. I had never been in a bra section alone, sports or otherwise. I didn't know what to expect.

As we walked away, Luke looked at Charlie and said, "This place still stinks. You guys don't even have a Starbucks."

Charlie narrowed his eyes, but didn't say anything. We left them behind, an epic journey ahead of us.

"Charlie," Just Charles said. "I knew he was a jerk. Who goes by Charlie when you could be Charles?"

While Charles continued his diatribe, I stopped dead in my tracks. I held my hand out in front of him, keeping him from mindlessly entering the dreaded sports-bra section.

"What's wrong?" Just Charles asked.

"We need a plan. We can't just walk into the sports bra section willy nilly," I scoffed.

Luke shrugged. "It's just fabric."

"For boobs," Just Charles said.

We all giggled. Yes, we were graduating middle school and moving on to bigger and better things, but we were still guys. And all guys, even my father's ripe old age, giggle about boobs. I'm not sure about Dr. Dinkledorf, though. If you ever meet him, be sure to ask him.

"We can do it. Together, gentlemen," I said. "On three."

Just Charles took a deep breath and did the sign of the cross.

I started the countdown, "One. Two. Three."

We walked together into the sports bra section. "Stay together," I said.

We walked slowly, eyes straight ahead, hoping Bryce would happen into our path.

"There he is," I whispered. I nodded to the hulking dude who seemingly had no problem that he was organizing sports bras. He was inhuman. Our football team was doomed.

"Talk to him," Just Charles said.

I elbowed him. "You talk to him."

"No, you."

"Excuse me, Mr. Lawson?" Luke asked.

Bryce looked up at us, surprised that three adolescent dweebs were in the sports bra section.

"Gentlemen, I'm gonna have to ask you to leave this

section. Sports bras are a serious business. It's not a joking matter for the likes of you."

"No, we're not here for that," I said.

"I don't do autograph requests in the off season."

"Oh, we're not fans," Luke laughed.

Bryce looked like he was trying to choke Luke with his mind.

"But we'd like to be on the same team," I said, jumping in before he used his hands to end Luke.

"You guys think you're cut out for football?" Bryce laughed.

I nearly fell over laughing. "Not. At. All. But we hate some of the players on the Cherry Avenue football team just as much as you do."

Bryce threw a sports bra with frustration. "Ugh, don't get me started. I can't stand those guys. Nick DeRozan. And the quarterback, Warblemacher. I'm surprised his head fits into his helmet."

"And what about that Davenport kid?" I asked, egging him on.

"The worst. Speedy little butt face. Can't stand him, either."

"Oh, God. I hate his butt chin," I said.

"Tell me about it," Bryce said, shaking his head. "You guys have to put up with those clowns every day? We only play them a few times a year and I can't stand them."

"It's tough, man. Draining. I can barely make it out of bed in the morning. Those guys run the school with insults and gut punches," I said, laying it on thick. "I almost lost a spleen a short time ago."

"I've gone through two of them already," Luke said. I didn't think we had multiple spleens, but Bryce wasn't the intellectual type.

"Typical," Bryce said, shaking his head. "What can I do to help you? I'd love to punch that Warblemacher in the face."

Just Charles said, "Yeah, but if you do that, he'll know it was you and then you'll get in trouble. We have a better idea."

"I'm listening."

Luke said, "We were thinking of getting a horse farm to dump all their manure on Randy's lawn."

Bryce smiled. "You guys are stone cold. I like it. Gamers. If only you weren't such nerds. We need that kind of mentality on the Bisons."

"I'll take that as a compliment," I said.

Bryce scrunched up his face, thinking. "I don't know anybody at a horse farm. But, Woody works at that giant garden depot."

"Woody, like Sheriff Woody? From Toy Story?" Luke asked.

I just shook my head.

Just Charles asked, "Why did we bring him?"

"No," Bryce laughed. "Sam Woods. He's a receiver on our squad. I think his uncle owns the place."

"How much manure would they drop on someone's lawn if they got an order?"

"I'll find out. You guys have cash?"

"Not on us, but we can get some," I said.

"I'll be in touch," Bryce said.

"Thanks," I said. "This is gonna be awesome."

"Hey, guys? Just do me a favor. Don't tell any of those Gopher Girls that you saw me in the sports bra section."

"We're never going to speak of this again, but I might tell everyone that I saw Randy wearing a sports bra in the locker room," I said.

"Stone. Cold," Bryce said. "I'll be in touch."

14

The next day, I made my way through the school hallway, not sure if I still smelled like fish. It's a terrible way to live. Anyway, as I passed the open gym doors, I heard the booming voice of Mr. Muscalini say, "Davenport! A word."

I took a deep breath. I hoped he wasn't going to ask me questions about how to help him get a butt chin again. I turned and forced a smile.

"Yes, Mr. Muscalini?"

"I just want to say, good luck to you in your valedictorian battle. You have fought with honor. I wish you the best."

"Thank y-"

Mr. Muscalini cut me off with a shrieking scream, "Oh, God. She's coming!"

"Who?" I asked, watching Mr. Muscalini run back into the gym.

"Amanda Gluskin, the psycho!" he yelled, before diving behind a bunch of old gymnastics mats. Amanda once beat up Mr. Muscalini in a fit of rage, emasculating him in the cold-blooded Camel Clutch.

I turned around. "Amanda Gluskin, the psycho!" I yelled, directly toward Amanda Gluskin, the psycho.

Amanda's eyes widened, then narrowed.

Kids seemed to apparate like wizards, arriving out of nowhere, to surround me and the psycho.

"Fight! Fight! Fight!" they chanted.

"No fight. Nothing of the sort going on here," I said, backing up to the wall.

Amanda stepped forward, grabbed me with both hands by my shirt and lifted. I was pretty sure I was off the ground, but on the bright side, I looked taller.

Ditzy Dayna walked through the still-chanting crowd and said, "Hey, you really had a growth spurt."

"I'm gonna kick your butt, after I tell you how spectacular you smell," Amanda said, closing her eyes and relishing in my fishy pheromones.

I looked around for an escape route, but couldn't find any.

"Punch him in the face," somebody yelled.

Then everybody started yelling.

"Body slam him!"

"Camel Clutch!"

I offered a contrarian idea. "How about we just hug it out? You're a reasonable person," I lied. "I was just repeating what Mr. Muscalini said. I didn't mean it."

Amanda glared at me, seemingly becoming overwhelmed by all the conflicting advice being thrown at her.

I used that confusion as my chance. I raised my right hand in karate chop formation and thrust it toward her jugular with devastating speed and precision. Amanda's hands were too slow to block my attack. She let go of me, but failed to get her hands up to protect her exposed jugular. Plus, I was falling to the ground, which accelerated the speed of my karate chop. So, she did what any reasonable middle schooler would do in a fight. She turned her face toward my incoming chop and bit me. Hard. Like Grimm-wolf-the-Gopher-hard.

I crumpled to the ground while Zorch burst through the wild pack, holding Amanda back from completely devouring me. I once thought she might eat me in sixth grade. I was certain that if Zorch wasn't there holding her back, she would've done it right then. What can I say? I'm very sweet and hard to resist.

Randy had a different interpretation. He said, "Daven-fart got beaten up by a girl. Again."

I stood up and fixed my shirt that Amanda had so rudely wrinkled.

"What are you tryin' to say, Ricky?" Amanda said, through gritted teeth. She took a menacing step toward him.

Randy jumped back and then took off down the hallway. I laughed. Amanda eyed me with hatred. My laughter ceased immediately, replaced by a big gulp. And not the good kind from 7-Eleven. This was a fear gulp. No added sugar.

The crowd dispersed after they realized an adult was there and nobody else was going to get punched, karate chopped, or bitten.

"You okay?" Zorch asked. "You still smell fabulous, by the way."

"Thanks," I said. "For saving me. She really is a psycho. Your buddy, Mr. Muscalini, just left me."

Zorch shook his head. "Don't be too hard on him. He's still in therapy after Amanda got him in the Camel Clutch."

"I've already got Randy on my case. I don't need Amanda plotting my death."

Zorch nodded, thoughtfully. "You seen anyone with spray paint around here?" "No. Can't say that I have."

"What about Saran Wrap?"

"What? What the heck would someone do with Saran Wrap?"

"They're wrapping all the toilets. They wrapped the door in the teacher's lounge. Mrs. Hennesy almost suffocated on the way to her break! This place is devolving into chaos."

"Mayhem," I added.

"Let me know if you see anything out of the ordinary," Zorch said, running off to chase after some kid with spray confetti. "I hate spirit week!"

But my luck changed rather quickly. As I was walking out of the building to wait for the bus, my phone rang.

I almost didn't answer it. I didn't know the number, but then I thought it could be Bryce about the doo doo delivery. I put the phone to my ear and said, "Hello?"

"Hey, Austin. It's Bryce. You haven't told anyone about the sports bras, have you?" he asked, concerned.

"Of course not. I gave you my word. Is that the reason you called?" I asked, confused.

"No. I wanted to tell you that Operation Poo is a go." We both laughed at the poo pun. "You'll be receiving a phone call from Woody's Uncle Doug. Woody said he was a little skeptical, so be prepared, Mr. Warblemacher."

"For what?" I asked. "Mr. Warblemacher?"

But Bryce was already gone. And he wasn't kidding. My phone rang a few minutes later.

"Hello?" I said.

"Yes, hi. This is Doug from The Garden Depot. May I speak to a Mr. Warblemacher?"

"One minute, please," I said, like I was the nicest receptionist ever. I covered the phone, cleared my throat, and used my deepest voice possible. "This is Mr. Warblemacher."

"I just want to confirm a manure delivery. You say you want a whole truck load?"

"Yes. As much as you can pile on," I grumbled deeply.

"What time do you want it delivered?" Doug asked.

"In the middle of the night. As quietly as possible," I said. "I'd rather not wake the neighbors."

Doug said, "Wait, this is a residential address?"

My plan was seemingly unraveling. I had to think fast. "Yes. I, ummm, run a business out of my house."

"What kind of business is that?" Doug asked, curiously.

I scratched my head. "Umm, plants." I remembered Max's plant. "Bonsai plants!"

"You sound very excited about your business, sir. That's good. I love manure."

"I always say, 'you have to be passionate about what you do, whether it's plants or poo.'"

"Amen, brother. Wait, bonsai trees? Aren't they really small? What do you need so much manure for?" Doug asked, pointedly.

"Yes, bonsai trees *are* miniature trees. But I, ummm, have quite a lot of them. I run a…Feng Shui consulting business. Have you considered Feng Shui to improve your working environment and employee morale?"

"No, I haven't," Doug said, confused.

"No? Well, perhaps we can set up a meeting after this transaction is complete to go through the many benefits of Feng Shui in the workplace."

"That sounds amazing. I hope we can build a long-term relationship here. The Garden Depot would love to be your permanent poo producing partner."

"Let's see how you handle this delivery. Remember. In the middle of the night and quiet. And just out of curiosity, where do you get all that poo?"

"Horse farms," Doug said, simply.

"I knew it!" I yelled, out of character. "I, ummm, always like to learn more about business supply chains. I just love the smell of commerce in the morning."

Doug laughed. "You might not love the smell of this commerce in the morning. Well, I thank you for your business. And I assure you, we will not disappoint you. We hope for many orders from you for poo in the future!"

I didn't know how many more people I wanted to send manure missiles to, but I didn't want to blow my cover or disappoint Doug, who clearly loved manure. "I'm looking forward to a great pootnership!"

This was going to be lovely.

MUCH TO JAY PARNELL'S chagrin, he lived diagonally across the street from Randy. But for one short moment in time, that less-than-desirable location became a hot spot for our nerd crew. We had talked him into having a sleepover so we could see Randy's reaction in the morning.

Jay's bedroom sat above the garage, giving us a great look at Randy's presently-perfect front lawn. And his security cameras would allow us to relive it for years to come!

"Let's take shifts to watch out for the delivery," I said. "I'll take the first one."

Jay, Luke, and Ben all lay down on sleeping bags on the floor, while I sat on Jay's bed, leaning up against the wall, looking out at Randy's house. Just Charles joined me on the bed.

"I'm not tired, man," Just Charles said. "I'll join you for a bit."

"Too much sugar?" I whispered.

"No," he said, defensively. "Well, probably."

We sat there for a while without saying anything. The rest of the crew was fast asleep. Luke snored like an asthmatic penguin. It was a ridiculously annoying, high-pitched wheeze.

Just Charles said, "It stinks that we can't light it on fire."

"I know. It was too much. I'm already on the verge of being expelled. I don't want to serve prison time for arson."

"That's reasonable," Just Charles said. "Would've been cool, though."

"Totally," I said.

We watched out the window for a while, dozing off. I was jolted awake by the warning beep of a truck that was backing up.

"Guys," I whisper-shouted. "It's here." I hoped the noise wouldn't wake anybody up. I crossed my fingers, wishing that the neighborhood just thought it was the normal garbage trucks, even though it was an off day. Dang it. We should've planned this better. And then Randy's outdoor light went on above the garage.

"Uh, oh," I said, to myself, but then took a deep breath when I realized it was on a motion detector.

The boys woke up and joined me at the window.

"This is gonna be amazing," Ben said, shaking with excitement.

The dump truck did its thing and dumped a heaping pile of poo onto Randy's front lawn. I mean, it was the biggest pile of poo I had ever seen and possibly the biggest one ever. There were thousands of pounds of it. I felt bad for whoever had to scoop all of it out of the horse stables.

The truck drove off, leaving deep tire tracks in the grass as an added bonus.

We did a celebratory hug on Jay's bed. I almost fell off, but even so, it was better than all of our previous attempts to high five.

"Who has the next session?" Ben asked.

"I'll take it," Jay said.

"You sure?" Just Charles asked.

"It's okay," Jay said. "I'll take the next shift. I have some work to do."

"Yeah, you do," Luke said.

I looked at the two of them. "What's going on?"

"Nothing," Luke said.

"Yeah, nothing," Jay repeated. "I'm going to catch up on some reading."

I cocked my head at them.

"Just go to bed," Jay said. "I've got this."

"Okay," I said. I was pretty tired.

I woke up a few hours later and all was not okay, but I didn't know it at the time. I sat up from the floor and yawned. I crawled up to the bed and joined Luke, who was keeping watch.

"It's about to get awesome," he said, giddy.

I looked outside. The sun was just peeking out from behind the trees in the distance. Randy's dad would most likely be heading out to work in the next hour.

I looked outside and inspected our handy work. It was even more beautiful in the light. Yes, it was a ton of poop, but the idea of it was beautiful.

Jay, Just Charles, and Ben sat up.

Luke looked at Jay and asked, "Should we tell them?"

"Tell us what?" Ben asked.

Something caught my eye as I stared at our pile of poo. "What is that rope running from the poo?"

"That's kind of what we wanted to tell you," Jay said.

"The chemistry club got you a present," Luke added. "For your loyal service to the students in standing up for us all."

"What did you do?" I asked, shakily.

"We didn't do anything," Jay said. "Yet."

"Oh, God," Ben said, taking his turn at a look.

"What is the chemistry club going to do?" Just Charles asked, concerned.

"Oh, look," Luke said. "There's Chu and his brother now. They're gonna blow that thing sky high."

"I thought we decided that was a bad idea?" I shrieked.

"You did," Luke said.

A black Nissan sedan pulled up to the curb. The passenger door on the car opened up. Alex Chu stepped out, looked around, and pulled a lighter from his pocket. He headed toward the rope.

"No!" I yelled. I lifted the window and yelled to Alex, "Don't do it!"

Alex nearly jumped out of his skin. He looked up at us and exhaled.

"You'll go to prison. You think dodgeball is bad?"

That did the trick. Alex's eyes bulged so big, I could see them from across the street. He hopped back into the car and disappeared. Crisis averted. I rested my head on my arms, leaning on the window sill. That would've been so bad.

I took a deep breath and stared out to the street. I watched an old woman in a robe and slippers walk her pug while smoking a cigarette. She kind of looked like the dog, her skin weathered. "Remind me never to smoke," I said.

"Don't ever smoke," Ben said.

"Good one," I said, still watching the woman. And then before I could say a word, she flicked the cigarette onto Randy's lawn. She walked away, leaving behind a small flame that consumed the rope, inch by inch, heading toward the poop pile.

I took a deep breath, thought about the science of it all, and exhaled with relief. "Idiots. There's no way that's going to light. The flaming bags of poo work because it's the bag that goes on fire. I thought we were going to be in trouble."

Jay smiled and said, "Agreed, but I used my drone to douse it with a few pails of lighter fluid while you all slept."

My eyes widened. This was bad. Like really bad.

Luke smiled and said, "Surprise!"

And then a pop exploded, followed by the rooommph of the pile of poo catching fire. Red flames danced in the wind. I could've sworn I saw the old lady's eye brows fly over the Jay's house. I felt for her. I really did. I lost my beautiful brows earlier in the year, also a result of brainless youth.

"That is totally awesome and really bad at the same time," Ben said.

You know what I wanted to say, but I just couldn't. Aaah-hhh, farts was not even close to summarizing what had just happened.

15

As I'm sure you can imagine, mayhem ensued. We all jostled to get the first look at what had happened. Blue and orange flames danced atop the surface of a ten-foot pile of poo. I searched around Randy's house for damage. There appeared to be none. The flames had not spread. Relief overtook fear and then anger.

"You idiots! What were you thinking?" I asked.

"What? You don't like it?" Luke asked.

"That was pretty bad," Jay said.

"Don't worry. It's fine," Luke said. "Here comes Randy now!"

We all looked out the window to see Randy and his parents rush out onto the lawn, and then back away, holding their noses.

I chuckled. Randy looked around, embarrassed, as neighbor after neighbor ventured outside to check out the commotion. Within a few minutes, there was a firetruck and a first responder there, sirens and horns blaring. My old pals, Fontana and McGuire, bumped each other to be first to the scene. They were the guys who helped remove me from Sophie's doggie door with a year's supply of butter.

"Just enjoy it, man," Ben said. "This is gonna burn for hours." Ben patted me on the back.

I smiled and relished the moment. We had just pulled off the most epic flaming pile of poo, perhaps in the history of the world. First, the belly button lint. Now, this. Austin Davenport. 2x Guinness Book of World Records Holder. And that was just in the past week.

And then it all got so much better. McGuire and his crew unleashed a butt ton of water on the poo, not only extinguishing it, but blasting Randy and his family with wet poo.

"Surprise," I whispered with a smile.

Despite the commotion, we still had school. True, it was spirit week, and finals were done, so we didn't have to do much, but still. We got ready and ate breakfast quickly. We also got lucky. Taking Randy's bus after the incident was probably a bad idea, but thankfully, he was otherwise engaged.

At school, of course, everybody thought I did it. I walked through the Atrium. Word spread like wildfire. Sorry, poor choice of words. I got a smile and a "Dude," from Nate Winslow. A "nice job," from Adam Klein, and a "Daven-pooooort!" from some seventh grader that I didn't know.

And then I almost cried. Luke's neighbor, Sal, otherwise known as the Releaser of Rats, walked toward me. You might remember the simple misunderstanding we had, or more aptly put, his misunderstanding of what I wanted. Which was simply a *few* rats to be released in the teacher's lounge, which at that point, had been taken over by Randy and Principal Buthaire's Peer Review Council, his ring of spies and ridiculous rule enforcers.

Sal clearly didn't understand the definition of 'a few' and released a hundred or so rats into the school, which wreaked major havoc. This mishap also created a monster, as he learned that he took pleasure in doing such things, and did it again during the Trial of the Century, when I was almost expelled for stealing Grimmwolf, among other things. It's a long story.

So, you can understand my concern as he approached. I thought about running, but he locked eyes with me. I didn't want to be on his bad side. Amanda Gluskin was the only person whose bad side I liked less.

He leaned in and whispered to me, "I heard about your poo plot. Challenge accepted."

"What challenge?" I asked, concerned.

"I went with a hundred rats. You countered with a thousand pounds of poo. I'm going to have to answer your challenge."

"Dude, no. It wasn't a challenge."

"If you don't win valedictorian, I'm gonna flood the school with ten thousand feet of snakes in your honor."

"Please don't," I said.

"Trust me, it'll be awesome. So much better than last time."

"Umm, yeah that was lunacy," I said.

He smiled. "I know. It was crazy good." He laughed maniacally.

I didn't have time to stop that, as crazy as it sounded.

Sal continued, "I have to thank you. You inspired me to achieve my full potential. You ever think about being a guidance counselor?"

"Not really," I said, not sure that inspiring evil villains was in a guidance counselor's job description.

I shrugged off Sal. He wasn't my responsibility. And I relished in the joy of the day. I denied it all, but it felt good knowing that so many people were grateful for my take-down of Randy.

I stood in the Atrium, waiting for Sophie. I hadn't told her about it. I hoped she wasn't going to be mad, but someone else emerged behind me. Someone without cute dimples and bouncy brown curls.

"Well played, Davenfart," Randy said, in my ear.

I turned around. "Would you like a mint?" I asked.

"What are you implying?" Randy asked.

"Your breath stinks," I said.

Randy scoffed, "Whatever."

"What do you want?" I asked, against my better judgement.

"I wanted to congratulate you on a prank well played. I know you pooped on my lawn."

It was the one thing I'd never been accused of at Cherry Avenue. I thought it might be more exciting, but it was all anticlimactic after the belly button lint.

"As much as I'd like to take credit for it, I didn't poop on your lawn. Let's face it, I'm not the only guy who can't stand you. It's pretty much everybody in this school but you, Regan, and Nick."

"You got a small victory, Davenfart, but this doesn't change anything. You're still going down for the money scandal." Randy laughed, and then walked away.

I yelled back with the wittiest of retorts, "Am not!"

I met up with Sophie and Ben a few minutes later.

Sophie looked at me like my mother would have had she learned of the previous night's activities. "Really, Austin?"

I leaned in and whispered. "That was totally unautho-rized, right Ben?"

"We didn't know about the lighting, but Austin set up the delivery."

"Not helping, Benjamin," I said. I changed the subject. "I figured out how to outsmart Randy. I'm putting the money back into the box," I said.

"But we didn't take it," Sophie said.

"If Dr. D. doesn't know about it, he might think he miscounted and Randy will be exposed as a liar. Surely, they'll believe Dr. Dinkledorf over Randy," I said, not sure about that at all.

Ben said, "Why don't we just prove Randy stole it?"

"How?" Sophie asked.

They both looked at me. "I have no idea. Like none. It wasn't even my idea in the first place."

Sophie asked, "Do you really think we ought to do more sneaking?"

"Probably not, but Dr. D. doesn't have alarm bells on his drawers, so it should be pretty easy," I said.

Ben added, "He probably still has a flip phone."

Sophie said, "He might still use carrier pigeons."

That night, I raided my bank account, borrowed a few bucks from my sister, and scrounged under every couch cushion in the house. Stealthily, of course. I couldn't risk Derek knowing what I was going to do. My friends did the same. We came up with the fifty bucks we had been accused of stealing. I just had to unsteal it.

School had been reduced to a test here and there, a bunch of assemblies, movies, and spirit week nonsense like pajama day and yearbook-signing day. Perhaps, I'm just bitter because every time I was asked to sign a yearbook, I was reminded of the Davenfart mishap.

The next morning, we were all in the auditorium signing yearbooks when the bell rang. I saw Dr. Dinkledorf across the room. I knew I could beat him to his classroom, if he was even going there, and put the money "back."

I hustled out ahead of the crowd and made my way toward my old history room. It took me a little longer than expected, given that nobody had anywhere to go, so the crowds were pretty slow. Normally, under the threat of detention or perhaps even death, kids nearly ran to class out of fear. That day, the crowd just kind-of meandered through the halls.

I looked around for teachers and security guards, and any principals skilled in the art of Chinese throwing stars. The coast was clear. Although Ms. Pierre could've been in the shadows. I had to be quick about it.

I slid into Dr. Dinkledorf's room and hustled over to his desk drawer. I pulled it open and pulled out the lock box. It was pretty light. I shook it. There was nothing inside. I didn't know what to do. Clearly, he would know that he didn't miscount the money if I put it back. Plus, he might not even check, knowing that he already turned the money in.

But I didn't have time to be angry.

I heard Randy's voice say from out in the hall. "What did you want to talk to me about, Dr. Dinkledorf?"

"Shoot," I whispered to myself.

I looked around, trying to figure out where to hide. The window was closed and I didn't have time to open it and get out safely. Plus, I was on the second floor. Nerds don't do second floor window jumps. Well, at least do them and live to tell about them. I turned around to see Dr. Dinkledorf's closet in the corner of the room, under the Speaker of Doom. I got there as quickly as I could and slipped into it, just as Randy and Dr. Dinkledorf entered.

"It's a serious matter, I'm afraid," Dr. Dinkledorf said.

"Are you dying?" Randy asked, without concern.

Dr. Dinkledorf said, "Not that I'm aware of."

Randy said, "Oh, I just thought because you were really old."

Idiot.

Dr. Dinkledorf shrugged it off and continued, "I had the money box dusted for fingerprints."

I pushed open the closet door just a touch to see what was going on. Things were getting good. Dr. Dinkledorf lifted the box by a metal handle on top and placed it on his desk. "Do you know what I found?"

I wished I could see Randy's face. His back was to me, as he faced Dr. Dinkledorf.

Randy said defiantly, "Fingerprints."

Dr. Dinkledorf corrected, "*Your* fingerprints."

I pumped my fist, but in the tight space, I almost knocked myself out. I hoped they hadn't heard me in the closet. I stood as quietly as I could.

Dr. Dinkledorf continued, "Turn yourself in or I will."

"I didn't do it," Randy spat. "I told you, I saw Austin do it."

"Very well," Dr. Dinkledorf said. "But be forewarned that turning yourself in will be infinitely better than if I present this evidence to Ms. Pierre. Think about it."

Randy nodded and left the room. Dr. Dinkledorf placed the box back into his drawer and then exited the room. I waited a few minutes until things were quiet. I opened the closet door and promptly tripped, as I attempted to step out onto the floor. I crumpled into a heap of nerd with a groan.

The sound appeared to have attracted one Eugene Zorch. I rolled to my side and looked up at the ginormously-tall man who towered over me while I was standing, let alone while nerding out on the floor. He shook his head as he stared at me.

"I have many questions, but I will ask none," Zorch said.

"I'm grateful for that," I said, sheepishly.

16

I walked down the hallway and was almost knocked down by the main office door swinging open. Dr. Dinkledorf surged out with an energy I didn't know he possessed. At least not during this century.

"This place is mayhem!" Dr. Dinkledorf yelled, to no one in particular. "Common sense has left the building. The war has begun, Austin. Prepare yourself," he said, shaking with intensity.

"I've been battling for years, Dr. D."

"Well, now I am officially in the fight. I will stop at nothing until order is restored!"

SPIRIT WEEK WASN'T JUST a time for the middle schoolers to create mayhem. The high school kids still reveled in its creation as well. And as I've mentioned in the past, my sister's grade was quite good at it.

I was heading to Sophie's impeachment trial and I was on the verge of being late. My mother was puking her guts out. Again. I found it very inconvenient. Do you remember when she puked in my mac 'n cheese? It's just not right. Anyway, I was minding my business as I always do, walking through the Atrium, when I heard squeaky footsteps echoing toward me.

Before I even knew what was happening, I found myself amidst the chaos and hysteria of a duct tape tornado. The worst kind of duct tape attack I'd ever experienced. As you know, a duct tape tornado can strike at any time and without warning. Sometimes the attackers yelled, "Duct tape tornado!" in excitement, giving a bit of a heads up before they enacted the deadly taping technique, but usually one was already ensnared or at least surrounded in said tornado, giving little actual warning.

Duct tape ensnared me as the attackers swirled around me, alternating high and low. Within seconds, the two twisted, trespassing tornado turds had mummified me in one of man's most functional weapons of repair. I stood there, swaying back and forth in dizziness.

One of the tornado turds poked me in the shoulder with his pinky. "Boop," he said, like he was tapping a baby's little nose. And then he let out an evil cackle.

I willed myself to remain upright, but the duct tape was so tight around my legs, there was nothing I could do. I toppled over like the Leaning Tower of Pisa, except worse. I was the Falling Tower of Austin. I crashed to the ground. Sneakers squeaked away as I lay there, helpless.

I called for help for a few minutes, but no one heard my pathetic cries. After what seemed like forever, but was probably only a few minutes, I heard the click clack of a woman's heels, heading toward me.

"My savior!" I yelled, rolling to my side.

My excitement quickly faded when I saw the evil that approached.

"Well, lookey what we have here," Ms. Pierre said with a smile. "Quite the predicament."

"Can you get Zorch, please?" I asked, ignoring her pleasure.

Ms. Armpit Hair ignored me. "He's busy at the moment."

"Can you help me, please?"

She ignored my request. "On your way to the impeachment, I suppose? You need to think about whether or not you should confess to save Sophie from humiliation. That's the only way to save her. Interestingly enough, I win either way. It's wonderful when it works out that way, don't you agree?"

"I humiliate her all the time! That's what I do." It wasn't a great argument, but I didn't know what else to say.

"Do you confess?" Ms. Pierre asked.

"I didn't do it," I said, defiantly.

Ms. Pierre's smile disappeared. "Very well, Misterrrr Davenport. I always knew you were more zero than hero. Enjoy your stay. It looks kind of cozy. Like a weighted blanket or something."

"Yes, but the concrete floor is not all that soothing for my head."

"Well, enjoy!" Ms. Armpit Hair said, before walking away.

"Don't leave me here!" I yelled.

Ms. Armpit Hair waved to me without looking back. She called out, "I will!" And then laughed like she was the Wicked Witch of the West, who was probably her Grandmother or something.

I waited for Ms. Armpit Hair to be out of ear shot and

yelled, "Help! Help!" I needed to get to Sophie's hearing. But nobody came. I'd have to be my own hero, instead of a zero.

I thought for a moment. My best idea was to gnaw through the duct tape like Grimmwolf would do. I reared back and opened my mouth to attack. My head surged forward, as I let out a ferocious growl. And promptly knocked myself out on the cold, hard floor.

I don't know how long I was out for, but no one had come to my aid, which probably meant the trial was still in progress. I'd hate to think it ended and not one person helped me out. But I didn't have too long to think. I was late. Sophie was in the midst of her most difficult moment, and I wasn't there. I did what any person would do in my situation. I log rolled down the hall.

I rotated my body, shoulder over shoulder, rolling my way to the auditorium. It took a little effort to get going, but once I got some momentum, it was almost fun. Well, besides the dizzying urge to puke after rolling for a few minutes.

I was a machine. It is quite possible that I was a steam roller in a previous life. I made it to the double doors of the auditorium, rolling as fast I could. The only trouble was that I was rolling so fast, I couldn't stop. I put on the brakes, but without my hands to stop me, I continued to roll down the auditorium steps, past my friends, enemies, and some uninterested parties. Some of the kids just watched in wonder while others laughed. I added to the fun, letting out a variety of squeaks and groans as I landed on each step, making my way down to the front row. And the squeaks were coming from both ends, unfortunately.

I ended my fabulous entrance with a face plant into the stage. My brain rattled. My ribs ached. My spleen most definitely gone forever.

"Aaaahhhh, farts," I groaned.

Within seconds, a crowd surrounded me. Through hazy vision, I saw Sophie, Ben, Sammie, Zorch, Dr. Dinkledorf, and Rose Dumbleton. Randy's laughter echoed in the background.

"What happened?" Sophie whisper-yelled.

I said, barely audible, "Bad weather. Duct tape tornado." Emotional and physical pain surged through my body.

"You got duct taped again?" Sophie said, entirely too loud.

"Isn't it obvious?" I groaned.

Sophie nodded, "I guess it is."

"We'll take a five-minute recess," Ms. Pierre said from atop the stage, unenthused.

"That was one heck of an entrance," Zorch said. "Never seen anything like it."

"Yeah, dude," Just Charles said. "You were like a human burrito!"

I shrugged. Well, as much as you can shrug when you're mummified in duct tape. Try it some time. It's not easy. "I'd have preferred to swing in on a rope or something."

"Yeah, that would've been much better," Ben said.

"Can somebody just roll me home? I can't look at any of these people ever again."

"It's not that bad," Sammie said.

I rolled my eyes at her.

Sammie nodded. "Yeah, it's pretty bad, but you're Austin Davenport. You've bounced back from worse."

Ben added, "Yeah, this is just how you roll."

"Not helping, Benjamin," I said.

"Sorry. Poor choice of words," Ben said, smiling.

Zorch cut me out of my duct tape disaster.

"You totally farted in there," Just Charles said, holding his nose.

"Is that how you powered yourself?" Ditzy Dayna asked.

"Yes," I said. "It was fart powered."

I turned and took Sophie aside. "I have to tell you something."

"I don't think I want to know," Sophie said.

"Ms. Pierre saw me lying there, taped up. She left me."

Sophie's anger started to boil. "That's terrible."

"It gets worse. She told me that she would only let me out if I confessed to taking the money."

"She's going down!" Sophie said, pounding her fist into her hand.

"I'm going to do it," I said.

Sophie did a double take. "Wait? What?"

Ms. Pierre interrupted our conversation by slamming a gavel on the table. She was taking this whole thing a little too seriously. "Order! Order, I say! We will begin now!"

I looked at Sophie and said, "You'd better get back up there before she starts gaveling your fingers, one by one."

"I'm gonna gavel her face," Sophie said, stomping up to the stairs and onto the stage.

Sophie sat down in her chair next to her lawyer, Just Charles, and mouthed to me, "Don't do anything stupid. We've got this under control."

I nodded, as I took a seat in the front row. I looked over to see Randy smirking at me. I wondered if he had some sort of condition that caused him to smirk all the time. Is idiocy a condition? I vowed to research it, if I ever became a doctor. Well, after I solve spleens. I didn't even know if spleens were solvable, but I was going to dedicate my life to figuring it out.

Ms. Pierre slammed the gavel down on the table and said, "This court is now in session. The Honorable Ms. Ann Pierre residing."

Dr. Dinkledorf rolled his eyes.

I stood up and said, "I did it!"

Ms. Armpit Hair smiled and asked, "What did you do?"

I was about to answer, but Sophie interrupted me. "He farted. He's got a weak colon. Didn't you hear them coming down the stairs?"

I flushed red with embarrassment. I had hoped Sophie hadn't heard them.

Randy's upper lip curled. He called out from the front row, "Your colon sickens me, Davenfart. It sickens all of us."

A few people clapped. It was wrong. My colon never did anything to any of those people. At least as far as they knew.

Ms. Armpit Hair looked at me, confused. She said, "So, you're confessing to having a weak colon?"

Sophie's death gaze penetrated my soul. I blew her a kiss and sat back down, thankful to still be alive. I looked at Ms. Pierre and said, "Yes. Yes, I am. It's weaker than you could possibly imagine. I felt the need to tell everyone that."

I looked over at Sophie to see her head in her hands.

"The prosecutor will call its first witness," Ms. Pierre said, looking at Rose Dumbleton.

"I call Randy Warblemacher," Rose said, batting her eye lashes at him.

Randy stood up, nodded his head at me with a smirk, and whispered, "I'm going to destroy you, Davenfart."

Randy walked up onto the stage and sat down in a lone chair in front of a table.

Just Charles stood up and said, "Objection, your Honor!"

Ms. Pierre rolled her eyes. "This isn't TV, Mr. Zaino. And he hasn't even said anything yet."

"I object to Randy even being called as a witness! He is a known liar and a cheat!"

The crowd mumbled, seemingly not sure about what to make of such a cunning move.

Ms. Pierre said, "Overruled."

Sophie sat, her arms crossed in anger, as Rose stood up and walked over to Randy.

"State your name for the record," Rose said, sweetly.

"Randolph-"

"Nancy!" I interjected his middle name, to laughter.

"Warblemacher."

"No outbursts from the crowd our I will have you removed!" Ms. Pierre said, glaring at me.

Rose continued, "Tell us about the terrible crime you witnessed."

Randy looked at me with a wry smile before he began. "Well, I saw Austin by the good doctor's drawer. At first, I didn't think anything of it. He put some money into his pocket and then later I overheard him and Sophie laughing and talking about spending some newfound money on a dinner date. Sophie said something like, 'This school owes me a lot more than this. You should've stolen more.'"

I looked at Sophie. If she could crush Randy's particles into a less-than-fine sand, she would've.

"Anything else?" Rose asked, smirking.

Randy said, "Yes. It was like Sophie had told him to do it. She was the ringleader and he was working for her. He's weak like that. Just like his colon. It's a troubling characteristic throughout his whole being." Randy looked like he might puke.

Rose looked at Ms. Pierre and said, "The prosecution rests."

Ms. Pierre looked at Just Charles and said, "Counselor. The floor is yours. You can cross examine the witness now."

Just Charles stood up and nodded at Sophie. "We have

no need to cross examine the liar and cheat known as Randolph Nancy Warblemacher."

I pumped my fist, so excited that Nancy was taking off as his middle name. It was payback for three years of Davenfart. But then I realized, he chose not to question Randy. But why? It was a big mistake.

The crowd chatter grew.

Sammie whispered, "What is he doing?"

Ben said, "We gotta go for the jugular. Expose him."

Randy smirked at me the entire way down the stairs. Regan rushed over and engulfed him in a giant hug, like he had just rescued a baby from a burning building.

Just Charles continued, "I call Dr. Dinkledorf to the stand!"

"You can stop with the theatrics," Ms. Pierre said, unimpressed.

Mrs. Funderbunk stood up from the crowd and said, "This is the theatre!"

Only Mr. Gifford stood up in support of her. Mrs. Funderbunk sat back down and folded her arms.

Just Charles paced in front of Dr. Dinkledorf. "The money was in your drawer, was it not?"

"It was," Dr. Dinkledorf.

"Did it disappear?"

"Yes." The crowd groaned. "But then I found it."

The crowd chatter rose.

"Order! Order!" Ms. Pierre said, banging her gavel.

"Wait, you're saying that the money wasn't stolen?"

"That is correct. I misplaced it. Found it this morning under some papers in the same drawer. Must've got separated when I was counting it."

"How much money was it?" Just Charles asked.

"Fifty dollars. The same amount that had been reported missing in the first place."

Just Charles paced around the floor. "Dr. Dinkledorf, are you saying that Mr. Warblemacher lied about Austin and Sophie stealing the money?"

"Yes. I am," Dr. Dinkledorf said, simply.

"How certain are you that Austin and Sophie had nothing to do with the disappearing money?"

"I'm 100% certain that neither student stole any money. It's Randy that should be in trouble for making false accusations."

I looked over at Randy. His face was a shade of pale I hadn't seen before.

"The defense rests, your Honor," Just Charles said.

Ms. Pierre didn't move. She took a few deep breaths and then said, "Ms. Dumbleton."

Rose stood up and pointed at Dr. Dinkledorf. "How can you be certain Austin didn't steal the money? Did you guard the drawer 24/7?"

"No," Dr. Dinkledorf said.

The crowd let out a collective, "Ooooh."

Dr. Dinkledorf continued, "But the students don't have access to the drawer 24/7. And I already told you the money has been found. It was never stolen."

Rose ignored his comment. "Is it possible that with your old age, you may have missed the criminal act?"

"Anything is possible." Dr. Dinkledorf stared at Ms. Pierre. "She could actually figure out how to run a school. I truly believe that. I doubt it will happen, but I believe she is capable."

Ms. Armpit Hair's face morphed red and shook like the ground beneath a rocket ship before blastoff. I'd never seen her so angry. She stood up and yelled, "Your insubordination is inexcusable! I am submitting an article 22. You could lose your job, Dr. Dinkledorf!"

Dr. Dinkledorf didn't flinch. True, his reflexes weren't what they once were, but I was certain she said it loud enough for his old ears to hear.

"I will accept whatever consequences such a misdeed requires," Dr. Dinkledorf said, without emotion. He then smiled and said, "I guess you can end this trial now. The sham that it was."

Ms. Pierre swallowed hard and whispered, "The court finds the defendant not guilty."

I jumped out of my seat, as the crowd cheered. I ran up onto the stage. The rest of my crew followed, as we all engulfed Sophie in a giant nerd hug. I could feel Sophie's body shaking with emotion. Her wet tears seeped into my shirt.

As excited as I was for Sophie to avoid losing her presidency, feelings of revenge bubbled up inside me. I was going to go on the offensive against Ms. Armpit Hair. How, you ask? I had no idea. None.

AFTER THE TRIAL, we celebrated at Frank's. Our entire group sat around a large table, pizza and soda seemingly everywhere.

I wasn't in a festive mood, though. I yelled, "I want payback on that woman!" I pounded my hand into my fist. "Owww! Why do I always do that?" After the pain subsided, I asked, "What do we have on her? What are her weaknesses?"

Ben said, "None."

Sophie countered, "The school *is* falling apart."

"Let's get her on misappropriating the budget," I said, excitedly.

Just Charles said, "That's how they got Al Capone. Not murder. But tax evasion."

"That's all well and good, but how do we find out it's true?" Ben asked.

"Good point, Benjamin," I said. "We need hard proof. Budgets. Bank statements."

Just Charles asked, "How do we get that?"

I shrugged. "No idea. Like none."

"So, what do we do?" Sophie asked.

"I'm going to break into her office," I said.

"You tried that once and almost got caught," she said, concerned.

"True, but you have to admit the farting computer was a great idea," I said.

Ben didn't appear to agree. It hurt me to my core. "If I hadn't seen Butt Hair and your brother heading toward the main office, you could've been expelled. Sent to LaSalle Military Academy."

"But now I know better."

"He's got a point," Just Charles said. "Maybe Evil Chuck could help." Charles must've been sipping pretty hard on the sodas.

"He's too reckless," Ben said. "He has no control."

I nodded. "He's right. This has to be about precision."

Just Charles just shook his head.

I said, "We've been preparing for this for three years. Everything we've learned from breaking into the Butt Crack, Zorch's Lair, Grimmwolf's Vault, the Dragon's Keep, and saving C.T. at Comic Con will go into breaking into the Arm Pit."

"Can we add a dive roll?" Luke asked.

"Dive rolls are a must," Just Charles added.

I was flabbergasted. "Guys, they're already in. It's a requirement."

Luke said, "Okay, so an extra one?"

I nodded. "Definitely."

Ben raised his hand, tentatively. "I hate to be a downer, but did we actually learn anything from any of those encounters?"

"Farting computers are funny?" Just Charles said with a shrug.

I said, "We've learned that we take too much risk. We need to learn from what we've never had."

"What's that?" Sophie asked.

"This time, we need an inside man. We've never had one before," I said.

Sophie countered, "How about inside woman?"

"Even better," I said, catching up to Sophie's plan.

Luke asked, "Does she have a phone number?"

"What about Dayna?" Sophie asked, annoyed.

"Half the time, she calls me Larry," Luke said. "We've been together for months."

"You kinda look like a Larry," I said.

"I've never been more insulted in my life," Luke said, his hands on his hips.

Just Charles laughed and said, "Yes, you have."

"Back to the plan," I said. "My lovely girlfriend had an awesome idea. We need Mrs. Murphy on our team. She can get us in."

"Do you really think that's a good idea?" Ben asked. "She works for Ms. Pierre."

"She doesn't like APH. She loves me," I said, like they were idiots.

"That's debatable," Ben said.

"I'm very lovable, right, honey?" I asked Sophie.

"It depends on the day," she said, seriously, but then smiled.

I didn't find it very amusing, to be honest.

Sophie pinched my cheek. "I'm sorry. You're very lovable. And so cute."

All was right with the world. I was back in planning mode. "Do we need any hotdogs to test for lasers?" I asked, remembering our Grimmwolf mission.

"It couldn't hurt," Luke said, who was never one to turn down a hot dog.

Ben's eyes lit up. "How about some snacks?"

"I could always use snacks. If my blood sugar goes too low, I can't think straight. And I'm going to need all my brain power to get this done."

Sophie rolled her eyes.

"Any chance we can get a marauders map or invisibility cloak?" I asked, referring to two of Harry Potter's stealthiest possessions.

Sophie shook her head. "Muggles don't have it that easy."

Just Charles said, "Life would be so much easier if we went to Hogwarts."

Sophie asked, "Would it, though? Austin would be blowing everything up and you know he would get on the bad side of the Dark Lord from day one."

"That's how I roll. But I would crush potions," I said, smiling.

"Speaking of rolling, when can we make fun of Burrito Boy?" Sammie asked.

I shook my head, disappointed. "This is serious business here."

"So, how are we gonna get to Mrs. Murphy?" Ben asked.

"I'll go see her and throw on the charm," I said, raising an eyebrow and pushing out pouty lips, my most charming look.

"Looks like you're ready to make out with a duck," Luke said.

"Yeah, not sure that's gonna work," Ben said.

"What? That's my smolder. It's patent pending," I said, defensively.

The Smolder

My so-called friends laughed.

I shook my head. "I'll get it done," I said. "I'm going to go see Mrs. Murphy now.

"Make sure you don't cause any unsuspecting girls to pass out with that smolder," Sophie said, laughing.

I stood up and stormed away. "I'm never coming back." I took two steps and then turned around, returned, to the table, and grabbed a slice of pizza. I looked at the rest of them and said, "What I said before."

I STOOD down the hall from the main office, waiting for Ms. Pierre to leave for a few minutes. I had done a pass-by and saw that the light was on in her office, no doubt planning her next conference to Tahiti or Bali or something.

When the office door opened, I turned to face the nearest locker and began fidgeting with the combination. Out of the corner of my eye, I saw Ms. Pierre strut behind me, her Austin radar seemingly down for maintenance. I waited a few seconds and then walked into the office, seemingly undetected.

Mrs. Murphy looked up at me. I threw on the smolder. She furrowed her brow at me.

"Austin, you okay? You look like you're trying to kiss a duck."

My shoulders slumped. "I'm fine. It's a long story."

"What do you need? Did Ms. Pierre call you down?" Mrs. Murphy asked, concerned.

I shook my head. "No. I'm here on my own."

Mrs. Murphy looked even more confused than when she saw my smolder.

I didn't know what to say or how to say it.

"What is it?" Mrs. Murphy asked.

I thought it best to not incriminate myself. "Let's say a student wanted to prove that a principal was a bad person and said student needed to get into the principal's office to find incriminating evidence. How would said student do it most easily and without getting caught?"

Mrs. Murphy thought for a moment. "Interesting hypothetical question. You would need help from someone willing to risk everything for the betterment of the school."

I nodded. "It would have to be someone close to the principal, right?"

"Close personally. And physically."

"Like smoochie smoochie?" I asked, not sure where this was going.

"No, like physically located near the principal," Mrs. Murphy said with a chuckle.

"Oh, right. For hypothetical purposes, someone like you," I said. "Sitting right outside the principal's office and knowing the principal's whereabouts at all times during the day."

"Yes. Hypothetically speaking."

"What time might said student swing by?" I asked.

Mrs. Murphy said, "I would suggest students, as in two. It would make going through the files that much quicker and reduce the amount of in-office snooping time."

"Interesting."

"As for the time,11:40 and approach from the east side. Tomorrow would hypothetically be a good time."

"Had this not been a hypothetical situation, I would say that you have been very informative, and I will forever be grateful."

Mrs. Murphy smiled, but then quickly turned serious. "She never lets me in her office when she's not around, so if you touch something you better make sure it's back in its place. She's very particular. And watch out for the trip wires."

"She has trip wires?" I asked. I shouldn't have been surprised given her clandestine background, but for some reason, I was.

"Probably. Hypothetically speaking," Mrs. Murphy said.

I RETURNED to Frank's before the party was even over. I walked over to the crew with my best smirk. I'd learned a thing or two studying Randy over the years.

"What happened?" Sophie asked, excitedly.

"The smolder smoldered, baby," I said. "We've got an invitation for tomorrow at 11:40."

"Do you think she's setting you up?" Cheryl asked.

I laughed at the ridiculousness of the question. "Not possible. I smoldered, remember?"

"Did the smolder really work?" Ben asked, surprised.

I took a deep breath. "It was a small part of my charm." I leaned in and whispered, "I'll go through her folders and files tomorrow and see if I can download her computer files. She said we should have two people."

"I'm going with you," Sophie said.

"No," I said, firmly. "You just avoided impeachment. You can't risk more. This is between me and her. Three years of principal payback."

"I'll go," Ben said.

Sophie said, "He's a bigger klutz than you."

"Thank you?" I said.

"We stole Grimmwolf together," Ben said.

"And the soap from Zorch's Lair," I added.

"We stole the dragon's egg from the Dragon's Keep," Sophie countered. "And this is personal," she said, through gritted teeth. "I'm going to be there at 11:40 tomorrow, whether you like it or not."

I looked at Ben and shrugged. "I guess I like it. And I guess you're on fire alarm duty."

Luke laughed and said, "He said, 'doody.'"

Thankfully, Luke was not joining us on the mission.

Sophie and I stood outside the main office at precisely 11:40 A.M. after approaching from the east, as hypothetically instructed. I was properly hydrated and snacked up.

"You ready?" I asked.

"I was born ready," Sophie said. She was so pumped up, she nearly ripped the door handle off. It reminded me of when she Hulked out when she thought I kissed another girl in sixth grade.

"Easy," I said. "We need to leave everything exactly as it was."

We entered the office. It was quiet. There was a stack of papers so high on Mrs. Murphy's desk that blocked her view of anyone entering or exiting the room. Nice touch.

We slinked over to the Arm Pit. I took a deep breath and opened the door. I held my breath, not sure if poison darts or even machine gun fire would be heading toward us at lightning speed. Nothing. Sophie and I slipped into the office and then closed the door behind us.

And then I executed my good luck charm, the dive roll. I lowered my head and rolled, heels over head into the heart of the Arm Pit. It was a little bit more crowded than I remembered. My foot banged into Ms. Armpit Hair's Department of Defense chair, which threw me off course. I winced, as pain shot up my left leg, and fell to my side, crashing into the bookcase.

The bookcase shook and rumbled above me.

Sophie shrieked, "No!"

Only a ton of books toppled off the shelves, and pummeled me one after the other, like a cartoon. But there was nothing funny about this. The books (yes, I'm blaming it on the books) must've set off some sort of alarm that blared throughout the Arm Pit and main office.

"Austin! Are you okay?" Sophie asked, wading through the pile of books to uncover my newly decrepit self.

"Spectacular, Mrs. Davenfart," I said, delirious.

Sophie found me underneath the pile and said, "Come on. We have to go!"

Mrs. Murphy was at the door. "You need to go! Now!"

"I can't," I said. "My ankle." I grabbed Sophie by the hand. "This is goodbye, my love. You must save yourself and never look back!"

"No!" Sophie said, tearing up, but she knew I was right.

"Come on, Dear," Mrs. Murphy said, pulling Sophie by the hand.

Reluctantly, Sophie followed Mrs. Murphy out the door.

Relief eased my pained body. At least Sophie was safe.

There was still a chance I could get out the window. I had broken into The Butt Crack through Prince Butt Hair's window. It would hurt a lot, but maybe I could make it.

One by one, I pushed the books aside, and pulled myself up by the desk.

And then horror struck me like an axe in the woods on Friday the 13th.

Ms. Pierre's voice echoed through the main office. "Interesting meeting you here, Ms. Rodriguez."

Within a few seconds, she was inside the office, staring at me. Sophie and Mrs. Murphy looked on, distraught.

"What a surprise," Ms. Pierre said, with little surprise.

I picked up a book from the floor, nearly bursting my lumbar, and placed it on the shelf with a forced smile. "I'm not sure what happened. The books fell. I thought you might be hurt, so I came in here. Do you use the Dewey Decimal system or what? If we work together, we can get this place back in shape in no time."

Ms. Armpit Hair looked at me and smiled. "Mrs. Murphy, please begin the expedited expellation protocol."

Mrs. Murphy scratched her head. "Ms. Pierre, I don't believe there is such a thing."

"Well, figure it out!" Ms. Pierre said, angrily. She took a deep breath and said, calmly, "Under section C, provision 12 of the student penal code, it states that a students who commit crimes while on the verge of graduation are subject to an expedited expellation hearing. And that applies to this situation." Ms. Pierre smiled at me, happier than I'd ever seen her before.

Ahhhh, farts.

17

It was spirit week, but I had no spirit. I was on the verge of expellation. I had beaten it before, but this was different. I was caught red handed, entangled in the Arm Pit. I'd be shipped off to LaSalle Military Academy in the fall and Sophie to the Phoenix Academy, a fancy name for a place where troubled girls go to get a second chance. It was a place even Amanda Gluskin didn't want to go. She was the toughest kid at Cherry Avenue. But it was only Cherry Avenue.

The Phoenix Academy had the worst of the worst. And Sophie and her sweet smile and bouncy curls would be toast. It was the kind of place where the kids ate the radioactive beef stew because they thought it made them tougher. You know, until they got sick from radiation poisoning.

I had no interest in participating in the spirit week tug o' war match. First, I was a nerd. Second, I was in a real-life tug o' war. My crew and I sat out from the afternoon's festivities, trying to figure out how to proceed. The expellation hearing was only a day away.

"We've got nothing," Sophie said. "We were caught red-handed, breaking into the principal's office."

"Were we, though?" I asked. "As far as Ms. Pierre knows, we just walked in. An honest mistake."

"Except that you had to do your stupid dive roll and knocked over all the books, so it looked like we ransacked the place."

"Anybody could've made that mistake," I said, defensively. I never realized dive rolls had a downside before.

"What do we do now?" Ben asked.

"Not much. Dr. Dinkledorf is representing us. He wants us to plead the fifth."

SOPHIE and I sat at a table on the auditorium stage with Dr. Dinkledorf in between us. Our fate was about to be determined. Would I be shipped off to LaSalle Military Academy, destined to be the worst cadet ever in the history of military schooling? Would my sweet Sophie end up scarred for life by a bunch of juvenile delinquents at the Phoenix Academy?

Our families were there, with worried expressions on their faces. With a touch of livid mixed in. Except Derek. I think he was hoping I'd get expelled. There were some kids from the student government, including Rose Dumbleton, who was the Secretary of the class and also Cheryl Van Snoogle-Something's nemesis at the Gopher Gazette.

We did the pledge and sat down. Ms. Pierre remained standing, about to address the group. She stared at me, hatred in her eyes, and then cracked a sliver of a smile, perhaps plotting my demise.

And then out of the corner my eye, I saw a blur enter

from stage right, swinging onto the stage on a giant rope. It
was C.T. Walsh, author extraordinaire! I cringed, as C.T. let
go of the rope, about to make his landing. It wasn't that long
since I'd seen him burst through a door and nearly concuss
himself at Comic Con, so I was not overly optimistic about
this particular entrance.

The crowd burst out into cheers. I opened my eyes. C.T.
had landed on his feet. Even he looked a little shocked, the
handsome devil.

C.T. yelled to the crowd, "Boom, baby!" And then bowed
to the applause. He shrugged and said, "That went so much
better than I thought."

But things were about to get worse. I looked over to see
Ms. Pierre on her feet, in some sort of Kung-Fu stance. She
looked ready to kill. And C.T. was her target. I'd seen C.T.'s
fighting skills at Comic Con when he went toe to toe with

fellow fart-joke author and criminal, Jimmy O'Beans (currently awaiting trial for his misdeeds at Comic Con), and he was okay. C.T. was pretty decent when fighting nerds who sat around typing all day. Ms. Pierre was another matter.

She sprung from her stance like a jungle cat. Cartwheel, backhand spring (in heels, or course) and crescent kick grazing the tip of C.T.'s nose.

"Not the money maker!" C.T. whined. He threw his hands up, as Ms. Armpit Hair assessed his many weaknesses. C.T. said, "Please, don't hurt me. I'm here for the hearing. This is how I enter all rooms. Bathrooms are particularly challenging, given the water hazards, but I love a good challenge."

Somebody yelled from the crowd, "Who the heck is that?"

Ms. Pierre growled, "Who are you?"

"I'm C.T. Walsh."

"Should I know you?" Ms. Pierre said, circling C.T. like she was about to devour him as an afternoon snack.

"Should I know you?" C.T. scoffed. He then looked at Sophie and me, and asked curiously, "Should she know me?"

Sophie shrugged.

C.T. said, "Well, allow myself to introduce...myself. I am C.T. Walsh, author extraordinaire. The Shakespeare of Fart Jokes. The Sandwicher of Unsandwhichable Things. The Catcher of Corn Dogs. The-"

Ms. Armpit Hair interrupted, "Are you quite finished, sir?"

C.T. hung his head. "Yes," C.T. said, sheepishly. "I was kind of running out of titles to make up, anyway." C.T. looked over at his trusty assistant who stood off stage and nodded. "Kyle- make a note. I need a longer list of titles at my disposal in case I find myself in a similar situation."

"What is he doing here?" I mouthed to Ben.

"Book signing. I sent Kyle a message," Ben said.

"You invited him?" I asked, impressed.

Ben responded, "Why do you seem so surprised? I have a good idea from time to time."

"That you do, Benjamin. That you do."

A girl from the crowd said, "That C.T. is so handsome."

Another girl said, "Meh."

Mr. Landon, the board president, asked, "What are you doing here? That was a great entrance, by the way. You should've had a cape."

C.T. said, "Dang it! Kyle, you forgot to give me my cape. Unreal."

The crowd laughed.

"He's so funny," someone said.

Ms. Armpit Hair noticed the tide was turning in her unjust war against Sophie. "Why is he here?" she asked. "Besides to make a mockery of the process of expelling students?"

C.T. responded, "This is already a mockery. I'm just adding to it. That's what I do."

Mr. Landon furrowed his brow and asked, "You just drop in on school hearings?"

"In all honesty, I looked up into the sky and saw the C.T. signal. I came as soon as I could," C.T. said, sitting down next to Sophie.

"The C.T. signal?" the bald board president asked.

"Yeah, like the Bat Signal," C.T. said, like it was totally normal for a regular dude to swing into a middle school meeting via rope and suggest he was alerted by a giant light shining in the sky.

"I'm pretty certain that's not a thing," the board president said, annoyed.

"Sir, I pity you. I'm here, aren't I? I am here, right?" C.T. patted his arms and then gave himself a purple nurple. "Ouch!" He looked at the crowd and smiled. "Sorry, sometimes I attend events digitally."

Everyone laughed. Sophie rolled her eyes. C.T. looked at me and shrugged.

"Again, why are you here?" Ms. Pierre asked.

C.T. slammed his hand down on the table. "Asked and answered, your honor!" C.T. yelled. And then totally calm, "I'm sorry. I love courthouse dramas."

Mr. Landon ordered, "Answer the question or I'll have security remove you."

"There's no need for security," Ms. Pierre said, seemingly plotting C.T.'s demise behind the school.

"I'm a character witness. And *you're* all witnesses. I think this lady wants to kill me," C.T. said, pointing at Ms. Pierre. The crowd laughed.

"You say you're a character witness?" the board president said.

"I know Austin better than anybody," C.T. said. "And Sophie, too."

"Better than his parents?" Ms. Pierre asked.

"Not really, no."

Mr. Landon questioned, "His brother?"

"Probably not," C.T. said, no longer making eye contact with any adults.

"His girlfriend?" Mr. Landon asked.

"Negatory."

"Sister?"

C.T. said, "Again, I'm thinking no. Does he even have a sister? I think that's a trick question."

It wasn't.

Ms. Pierre asked, "What do we need a character witness for anyway? This is not about character."

"It's all about the characters," C.T. said, slamming his hand down on the table.

Dr. Dinkledorf said, "This is going poorly."

C.T. whispered to Sophie, "If this goes south, we'll smuggle you into Mexico and start up a taco stand in Guadalajara. The profit margins on guacamole are enormous."

Mr. Landon nodded to the crowd and addressed C.T. "Have a seat with the rest of the attendees. Your presence is not required on stage. We'll see if we need you."

C.T. stood up. "That hurts. I'm hurt. I may not recover."

C.T. walked down the stairs and up the main aisle. He stood in the aisle, waiting for Just Charles to stand up to let him pass. C.T. patted his own chest.

"Just Charles, my man! Chest bump!" C.T. thrust his chest at Just Charles, whose nerd reflexes were about five minutes behind.

Just Charles crumpled to the ground with a groan, and laughter from the crowd. C.T. gave a sheesh face and then helped Just Charles up.

The board president held his face in his hands. "Try not to concuss the children, Mr. C.T."

"Mr. C.T. I like the sound of that. And of course, a good rule," C.T. said, before sitting down next to Charles.

I whispered to Sophie and Dr. Dinkledorf. "We need to call C.T. to the witness stand. He's our only hope."

"I was thinking the truth was our only hope," Sophie said.

"But we did actually break in," I whispered.

"Oh, yeah," Sophie said. "I forgot we actually did that

one. Can you blame me? It's ridiculous how many false accusations there have been over the years."

"You're telling me," I said.

Dr. Dinkledorf interjected, "You have to plead the fifth," referring to the Fifth Amendment, which states that when charged with a crime, a defendant has a right to remain silent and not rat him or herself out.

Dr. Dinkledorf stood up. "My clients plead the fifth."

The crowd chatter rose. It appeared as if people were surprised.

"Did they really do it?" somebody asked.

"That seems suspicious," another said.

"The tide is turning away from us. We need a distraction until I can think of something," Dr. Dinkledorf said.

He looked into the crowd at C.T., whose head was bobbing up and down, seemingly asleep.

Dr. Dinkledorf stood up and ceremoniously stated, "I call C.T. Walsh as my witness."

Just Charles nudged C.T., who startled awake.

"Dude! I was meditating."

"They want you on stage," Cheryl said.

C.T. said, "Of course, they do. Thank you, Ms. Van Snoogle-Something."

He stood up and walked up onto the stage. As he passed Ms. Pierre, C.T. said, "That cartwheel was pretty sweet. Can you teach it to me sometime?"

Ms. Pierre narrowed her eyes at him and said, "I'll pummel you with it."

"All righty then," C.T. said, sitting down in a chair separated from the rest, seemingly like a witness stand.

Dr. Dinkledorf stood up and paced around the stage. "Please state your name."

"Chadwick Theloneus Walsh."

"Is that your real name?" Mr. Landon interjected.

"As far as you know," C.T. said, winking at me.

Mr. Landon asked, "Do you have a birth certificate?"

"I am the proof of my birth. I don't think I deserve a certificate for that. My mother did all the work. I think we give out too many trophies and certificates solely on the basis of participation. It's not right."

Mr. Muscalini led a round of boos. He was big on ridiculous trophies.

Dr. Dinkledorf asked, "You are here as a character witness, are you not?"

C.T. smiled. "I am."

"How do you know Austin and Sophie?"

"They helped me save the world last summer. They saved my career from the evil clutches of that fraud Jimmy O'Beans."

"Relevance?" Ms. Pierre called out to no one in particular.

C.T. ignored her and said, "Austin is a good boy. He would never have broken into the principal's office." He stood up and raised a pointed finger. He said, angrily, "I'll tell you who's to blame! It's that Randy Warblemacher!"

"Sit down, Mr. Walsh," Mr. Landon said, rolling his eyes. "This is not an episode of Judge Judy."

C.T. sat down. "Is anybody taping this? I *would* like to watch it," he said, eagerly.

C.T.'s question was ignored. "That is quite an accusation," Ms. Pierre said.

"Indeed," the board president said. "Based on what information?"

C.T. said, simply, "Austin told me he's a jerk. That should be good enough, right? This isn't a real court or anything."

"But witnesses put Austin and Sophie inside the principal's office when the alarm bells went off," Ms. Pierre said.

"Oh, really?" C.T. asked, surprised. He shook his head and said, "Inconsequential. What I want to know is what is the principal hiding that she has to have an alarm on her office?"

Chatter arose in the crowd.

Dr. Dinkledorf looked at Mr. Landon and Ms. Pierre. "This is my witness. I'll do the questioning."

C.T. continued, "Maybe *she* should be the one who's on trial? Let's expel *her*. See how she likes it."

The crowd cheered. Nobody really knew what to say. C.T. was making such a mockery of the process, confusion was taking over.

C.T. said, "You guys should really have food vendors at these things. You could get a lot of extra money for clubs and stuff. The corn dog money alone should be enough to start a C.T. Walsh fan club."

"Is that all?" Mr. Landon asked, seemingly unimpressed.

C.T. looked over at the board president and said, "Only this." He exploded out of his chair and thrust his first into the air. "Set Austin and Sophie free!"

The crowd cheered. Nobody stopped to think that nobody was, in fact, a prisoner. But that didn't stop us. Everyone bounced out of their seats, yelling and high-fiving each other. Or at least they tried. Just Charles smacked Tracy Dunleavy in the face while attempting to dodge Ben's ballistic fist.

"They're not imprisoned," Ms. Pierre said. "Yet."

"Yeah, but what rhymes with expellation?" C.T. asked.

"Is that even a word?" Mr. Landon asked, his eyes narrowing.

"I'm an author. Don't question my wordsmithery." C.T.

looked over at Kyle, excitement in his eyes. "Kyle- write that down! I'm the Wizard of Wordsmithery!"

"Enough playing around," Ms. Pierre said. "This isn't a courtroom. It's a hearing. I will conduct it as I choose."

She walked behind me and whispered, "I hope you've had your fun. Once Mrs. Murphy gets on the stand, it's gonna be all over for you."

"We'll see about that," I said, not sure what Mrs. Murphy was actually gonna say.

Ms. Pierre said, "Dr. Dinkledorf, do you have any substance to your argument?"

Dr. Dinkledorf pulled the beard on his chin anxiously. He paced around the stage, looking out into the crowd. And then I saw his eyes connect with Mrs. Murphy. I couldn't read her expression. I was nervous. What would she tell them? She knows we did it. But she helped us. Would she rat us out to save herself? I shuddered at the thought. Of that, and for thinking of rats in the auditorium, remembering Sal's rat assault last year.

Dr. Dinkledorf straightened up. "I call Mrs. Mary Murphy to the stand!"

Sophie looked at me, eyes wide. "What is he doing? If she tells the truth, she'll lose her job and we'll be finished," she whispered.

C.T. walked back to his seat, attempted to high five Just Charles, but missed, and sang, "Crushed it!"

Mrs. Murphy stood up from the crowd and made her way to the stage. The crowd was just as confused as Sophie and I, and perhaps even Dr. Dinkledorf. Had the old man finally lost his amazing wit?

Mrs. Murphy sat down. She avoided eye contact with everyone on the stage.

Dr. Dinkledorf said, "Did Austin Davenport and Sophie

Rodriguez enter Ms. Pierre's office on the morning in question?"

"Mayday. Mayday," I whispered.

Mrs. Murphy paused and looked at Ms. Pierre then us. "Yes."

The crowd groaned. My heart sank. My mouth went dry. It finally happened. The less-than-dynamic evil principaling duo of Butt and Armpit Hair had taken us down. Sophie wiped a tear from her eye.

But then Mrs. Murphy continued, "But they didn't break in."'

"They didn't?" Dr. Dinkledorf asked, almost as surprised as the crowd.

"I must've made a mistake. I called them down to the office. I'm typically inundated with requests. Dozens of call-downs a day. And Austin is called down more than any student.

"Nice work!" Derek called out.

My father elbowed him.

Mrs. Murphy continued, "I must've forgotten to throw out an old slip with Sophie's and Austin's names. They came down, as called. Some books in Ms. Pierre's office must've fallen, setting off the alarm. The children, being the wonderful students and citizens that they are, rushed into Ms. Pierre's office to see if she was okay. They didn't know she wasn't there."

Ms. Armpit Hair's face boiled red. She nearly shot daggers out of her eyes at Mrs. Murphy.

Dr. Dinkledorf seized the moment. "Were there any other witnesses there?"

Mrs. Murphy smiled. "There were not."

Dr. Dinkledorf said, "Mrs. Murphy is an esteemed member of this staff. She was the only witness to the alleged break-in, which she claims never happened. The defense rests."

Dr. Dinkledorf sat down to applause. Sophie squeezed my hands. We continued to hold hands, waiting for our fate to be determined by the less-than-godly masters of our school universe, the board president and Ms. Armpit Hair.

Mr. Landon said, "Well, without any other witnesses or evidence, this hearing is over. Austin Davenport and Sophie Rodriguez remain students in good standing. Good luck in high school."

Ms. Pierre shot up from her seat so fast, her metal chair toppled over behind her, and landed with a clank.

Sophie and I jumped up and hugged. Dr. Dinkledorf joined in. He smelled kind-of like mothballs, but I was too excited to care.

My parents, along with Sophie's, rushed over to us. C.T. was not too far behind. I hugged my parents. It was quite awkward, as my mother's pregnancy stomach pushed mine back, and I ended up butt-bumping Mr. Rodriguez.

"Group hug!" C.T. yelled, engulfing my parents on the outside.

Dr. Dinkledorf said, "Justice has been served! Or not served. I've never been clear on that when the people are innocent." He tapped his chin. "But you weren't innocent. But it wasn't fair. Hmm," he said, thinking.

"Get in here, ya old coot!" C.T. yelled, pulling Dr. Dinkledorf into the hug. We hugged for another few seconds and then C.T. said, "Okay, this is getting awkward. I don't know most of you."

Sophie hugged C.T. She looked up at his kind, hand-some face and said, "Thank you so much for coming. I think."

"When I heard you were in trouble, I got here as soon as

I could. Kyle forgot my cape, but whatever. I sticked the landing, so I'm not going to be too hard on him. Is it sticked or stuck the landing? Whatever. I nailed it."

"When are you gonna lay off Kyle about the cape?" I asked.

"When he gets it right."

"Capes aren't everything, C.T.," Sophie said.

"I guess there *is* a downside to capes. It could've messed with my aerodynamics."

"Yes," Sophie said. "The greatest superhero costume creator ever, Edna, Mr. Incredible's personal fashion consultant, hates the use of capes."

"But they look so dang spectacular," C.T. said, envy seeping from his pores. He held out his hand for a shake. "Hold onto this one, Aus," C.T. said, nodding at Sophie. "She's a sane voice in the insane world of us caped crusaders. Or those wanting to be a caped crusader. Time for me to make my exit. I need a cool exit." He thought for a moment. "I got it! I'm totally getting exploding smoke bombs to disappear! How sick will that be?"

"Pretty sick?" Sophie said, unsure.

C.T. bounced up and down, clapping like a giddy little kid on Christmas morning. "I enter to great fanfare via the rope swing and exit with mysteriousness via the smoke bomb! It's genius."

I couldn't argue with that. I looked at my parents, who were a little less sure than I was.

"Hey, Aus. Do you think we could whip one up in the science lab before I leave?"

"I don't know," I said. "I'm kinda short on time." Plus, I didn't feel like blowing up the lab during unauthorized time. It was totally allowable to do it during an actual science class, but sneaking in to make stuff that ends up blowing up? Immediate expellation.

"Oh, I get it," C.T. said, disappointed. "I need a corn dog to ease my sorrows."

"There's food outside," my mother said. "I had a craving for nachos."

C.T. looked at me and whispered, "Your mother loves nachos? You are the luckiest kid in the world."

I wasn't certain that I was the luckiest kid in the world, nor that nachos made it so, but I agreed, nonetheless.

We walked out of the auditorium to find Calvin Conklin standing outside in mid broadcast. "The people have spoken today. Author C.T. Walsh flew in, literally, to save the day. He's a very handsome man, Ted. Don't you think? Meh? Meh? Ted, you're dead to me. Are you even *real*, Ted? I don't remember ever meeting you in person. You sit next to me in the morning meeting every day? Are you the bald guy with the handlebar mustache?" Calvin yelled, excitedly. "Ted, can we do a segment on mustaches?"

Sophie and I just kept walking, laughing uncontrollably.

"Good old, Calvin," I said, wrapping my arm around Sophie.

"Never a dull moment," Sophie said.

"It's mayhem around here. All day. Every day."

Dr. Dinkledorf caught my attention. I walked over to him.

"Thanks for your help," I said. "I think. How did you know Mrs. Murphy would cover for us?"

"I didn't," he said, simply. "I had a hunch."

"You gambled my life on a hunch?" I asked, confused and angry.

"It seemed like a good idea at the time. No harm. No

foul. Right?" He slapped me on the shoulder, and nearly knocked himself over.

"I need to take down Ms. Pierre," I said.

"You and me both," Dr. D. said.

"I know she's stealing from the school, but how do we prove it?"

Dr. Dinkledorf smiled and said, "Fwahhh!"

"Huh?'

"The F.O.I.A. Freedom of Information Act. Request the budget. Expenditures."

"Yes! We'll comb through those documents like my brother combs his non-existent mustache!"

"Does he do that a lot?" Dr. Dinkledorf asked, confused.

"Yes!" I yelled.

"Then yes! Do that!" Dr. Dinkledorf said. "You'll have to make a formal request through the board of education."

ON THE WAY OUT, I bumped into the board president. Literally. Both of us were looking down at our phones when we collided. I bounced off his fluffy belly with a manly "Flurf!"

"Oh, Austin. I'm so sorry. Are you okay?"

I didn't want to tell him that he was soft as a baby's butt.

"Fine," I said.

"Interesting afternoon," he said. "I thought that C.T. guy was going to ruin the whole thing."

I chuckled. "Yeah, that's how he rolls."

"Handsome man, though," Mr. Landon said.

"Meh," I shrugged.

"I loved the corn dog idea."

I nodded, enthusiastically. "I think people want to eat more corn dogs. They just have a hard time finding them.

Bring corn dogs to the people and you will have happier people."

"And more money for the school," the board president added.

"We could use it. If the world ran out of duct tape, the whole school would fall apart."

Mr. Landon's eyes widened in shock. "Don't you dare say that. My grandmother used to say, 'without love and duct tape, the world would fall apart.'"

I wasn't certain of that, but I did realize the importance of duct tape. "Maybe we should sell corn dogs to buy duct tape. Or just put more money in the budget for duct tape."

"All fabulous ideas, Austin. I do often wonder where a lot of the budget goes," the president said, scratching his head.

"Aren't you the board president? Shouldn't you know where the money goes?"

"Yeah, of course. I was only kidding," he said, totally not kidding.

"Can I ask you a question?" I asked.

Mr. Landon nodded. "Of course. Anything."

"I've always loved numbers. And I think it's really cool what you do, too."

"Well, thank you."

"How can I learn more about the budget? I mean, where would I go to find the budget and read about it and learn how the money is spent? Somebody mentioned I should Fwaaah it up or something."

Mr. Landon laughed. "Yes. The Freedom of Information Act. Fill out the paperwork and I'll get you the stuff over the summer."

"Umm, how about by tomorrow? I'm so into it. I just want to dive right in," I said, enthusiastically.

Mr. Landon shrugged. "Well, I probably could have Mrs. Dithers scrape up something. I'll have her leave it in the office for you." He slapped me on the shoulder. "Glad things worked out for you."

Fingers crossed. And my legs. I had to fart and didn't want to do it in a main area.

THE NEXT DAY AT SCHOOL, I stood with Ben, waiting for everyone to arrive for another fabulous day of spirit week. The Speaker of Doom crackled to life. Ben mocked, "Austin Davenport to the principal's office."

I laughed until the Speaker of Doom boomed, "Austin Davenport to the principal's office."

"Now what? Somebody better be dead," I said, angrily. Well, I really hoped nobody was dead, but there better be a good reason other than me being harassed by Armpit Hair.

I grabbed my stuff and headed down to the main office. I stopped dead in my tracks. I looked down and checked my belly button for lint. Clean as a whistle.

I walked into the office and again stopped dead in my tracks. Nobody was dead, but it did look like a bomb went off. Boxes and boxes were stacked on top of each other, scattered all about. There were so many boxes, there was barely a walkway to all the offices.

Ms. Pierre stood in the archway of her office door, seething.

When she saw me enter, she shot lasers from her eyes into mine.

"What?" I asked. "Do I got a boogie?" I wiped my face without waiting for an answer.

She said through gritted teeth, "Get this stuff out of here

now or you'll be a dead man. You've got thirty minutes. Tick, tock, bang."

Aaahhh, farts. I had no idea what she was talking about. Well, other than she was plotting my demise. I wasn't about to ask her for clarification. Thankfully, she turned and slammed the door behind her, disappearing into the depths of the smelly Arm Pit.

Mrs. Murphy looked at me with eyes wide.

"What is she talking about?" I asked, confused.

Mrs. Murphy said, "These are the papers you requested."

"I didn't request any papers."

"Yes, you did. The FOIA request for budget information."

My eyes widened. "Oh. My. God. What the heck am I gonna do with all this? How am going to get it home? Do you think I can take this home on the bus?"

"That's probably not going to happen," Mrs. Murphy said.

I thought for a moment and then yelled to no one in particular, "The Zorchmobile!"

Mrs. Murphy said, "Huh?"

I didn't have time to explain. I turned and bolted from the main office.

"What about the boxes?" Mrs. Murphy called after me.

I went straight to Zorch's Lair. The door was partially opened. I was so excited, my knock nearly blasted the door off the hinges.

"Whoa!" Zorch said, annoyed. He met me at the door. His face softened. "Oh, Austin. What's going on?"

"I need to borrow the Zorchmobile."

"What? What the heck is the Zorchmobile?"

"That's your car? I thought everybody knew that," I said, surprised.

"Nobody knows that."

"Well, now we both do. And I need to borrow it."

Zorch said, "Austin, you can't drive my car-"

"The Zorchmobile," I corrected.

Zorch rolled his eyes. "You can't drive the Zorchmobile in eighth grade."

"I didn't say I was driving. We need to move or I'm a dead man. Oh, and bring one of those cool dolly things."

"What are we transporting?" Zorch asked. "It's not stolen, is it?"

I scoffed. "No. It's just me. Then a bunch of boxes."

Zorch shook his head. "You're not riding on the dolly. It's an insurance liability. And do you even have your mother's permission?" Zorch asked.

"Of course not," I said with a smile.

"Get it and then we go."

"Can I ride on the dolly?" I asked, enthusiastically.

Zorch's shoulders slumped. "I guess so."

"Yes!" I pumped my fist.

18

We assembled in our Anti-Armpit Hair Lair, otherwise known as my basement. The high from my dolly joyride was long gone. I stood in between Ben and Sophie with Just Charles and Cheryl, staring down stacks and stacks of papers.

"How are we going to go through all this?" Sophie asked.

Just Charles scratched his head. "I'm a nerd and I don't want to read all this stuff."

"We're never gonna find anything in all of this. It's like a mouse fart at a Goat Turd concert," I said, lost in thought.

"Huh?" Sophie said, turning to me.

"I thought I was being perfectly clear." I thought for a moment. "What if we don't have to read any of this?"

"Then nothing happens," Ben said. "And evil wins."

"We can outsource it," I said.

"Who is gonna read all this before graduation?" Sophie asked.

"Not who. What," I said.

Sophie rolled her eyes. "Will you stop trying to be all mysterious and just tell us."

I shrugged. "I guess. But that's less fun. We build or find software that can analyze the data for us, looking for key words, discrepancies. And then we dig in from there."

"Not bad," Just Charles said. "We've got to do a little research."

"We're still gonna need a bunch of scanners. I have a wireless one upstairs," I said.

Sophie added, "I'm sure I can bring one over."

"Me, too," Ben said.

I nodded to Just Charles. "Can you start researching the programming? Or build one by the time the pizza gets here?" I asked, laughing.

"I'm good, but I'm not that good. I'm sure we can find something online."

And we did. By the time the Revengers had assembled with our scanning weapons, Just Charles had started a free trial of a program called Scanjitsu, like ninjitsu, but for scanning. It was perfect. We would use scanning technology with the art of stealth, and reveal Ms. Pierre's own stealthy and criminal tactics, if they actually existed. If not, at least my dad was going to get us pizza. With middle school winding down, my nerd self kicked in (you're probably wondering if it ever shuts off) and I wondered if it would've made more sense to just buy Frank's, given all the pizza we bought in the past three years. It was a project for another time.

"Boom, baby," Just Charles said, after synching the final scanner. "I've set the programming to pick up certain keywords and payment frequency. My dad said we could look up companies we come across using some of the legal subscriptions he has at work."

"Nice. Extra pepperoni for you," I said, patting Just Charles on the back.

"How about an extra soda?" he asked with a raised eyebrow.

We all said, in unison, "No!", remembering the time when we had to strap Just Charles to my basement couch after he went haywire, turned into his heavily-sugared alter-ego, Evil Chuck, and commandeered my tree house. We let him off easy, because he didn't take any squirrels hostage, but still, it was bad.

I'll save you the boringness of the scanning process. While we fed ourselves pizza, we each had a scanner that we fed thousands of pages of documents each. And then it burped out a bunch of information for us.

"What do we got, bro?" I asked Just Charles.

"Heartburn," he said, chewing on his third slice.

Cheryl shook her head. "I don't know how many times I have to tell him to stop at two."

"It's pizza," Ben said, like his answer made total sense.

Sophie said, "I think he was asking about the Scanjitsu results."

"Ahhh, right." Just Charles navigated the program with a few scrolls and keyed in words. "There is quite a bit of airfare expenses, but even more than that, there are about a hundred payments to the Cayman National Bank. And Zurich Bank."

"That's in Switzerland," I said, rubbing my frustratingly-flat chin.

"What does that even mean?" Sophie asked.

Footsteps creaked down the basement steps, which was a frequent occurrence when the orchestra of smells made their way up the stairs, calling out to all within smelling distance. Thankfully, it was my dad and not Derek.

"Cayman and Swiss banks? Don't you think you're a little young to launder money?" my dad asked with laughter.

"Is it normal for a school to make payments to international banks? Like a lot of them. Asking for a friend," I said.

Dad shook his head. "I'd have to say negatory. What are you guys doing, anyway?"

Cheryl answered, "Just helping with some research for a school newspaper story."

My father frowned, then shrugged.

"Can we help you?" I asked.

"Oh, right," he said. "I'm the Quality Control Supervisor here. Just want to make sure this pizza is up to snuff." My dad grabbed a slice and slapped it on a plate.

Dad disappeared with a smile.

Just Charles looked at me. "Now what?"

"Now we expose her," I said.

"How?" Sophie asked.

I smiled. "I have just the idea."

19

I t was graduation day. I stood with Ben, Just Charles, and Luke, our black gowns making us look like a bunch of doofuses. We stood together in the Atrium outside the auditorium. Parents were talking while kids were making their way to the band room, where we would all congregate before walking out onto the stage. While no one was looking, we snacked on the after-graduation refreshments.

"What happens if this goes south?" I asked.

"Pull the fire alarm," Ben said. "That can get you out of most middle school problems."

It did save me one time when I was trapped in The Butt Crack, Principal Buthaire's old office, under his desk. I had wiped his computer clean of security camera tapes and may have drawn a mustache on his wife's picture, and added a fart noise every time he got an email. It's never been proven that I was the perpetrator, however, because Ben saved me by pulling the fire alarm.

"Sounds like a reasonable escape plan," I said.

"Mmm, hmmm," Just Charles said, a whole brownie in his mouth.

"Dude, relax. We don't need Evil Chuck ruining our big reveal."

Just Charles frowned and said, "Rom ofrranded."

"What did he say?" Luke asked.

Ben and I shrugged.

"We should make our way to the band room," I said. "But I have one thing to take care of," I said, looking across the room at Zorch.

Little did I know at the time, but Just Charles had hidden a stack of brownies beneath his flowing graduation gown and would ingest them in secret.

I WALKED UP to Zorch and Mrs. Zorch, formerly Ms. Geller, the head of our crack cafeteria staff. Many have questioned whether the food actually came from someone's butt crack before making it onto our trays. It usually tasted that way. I smiled as I approached.

"Austin! Congrats," Zorch said, straightening his clip-on tie that sat atop his white short-sleeved shirt.

"You look good," I said.

"Doesn't he?" Mrs. Zorch said.

"I feel like a limo driver," he said, grumpily. "Anyway, congrats. And good luck with the valedictorian thing."

"Thanks," I said, shaking his hand.

Mrs. Zorch asked, "So, Austin. Would you like my catering company to take care of the food for your graduation party? I'm working on some new things."

"Oh, God no," I said, without thinking. "Umm, I mean, I'd hate for you to have to go through the trouble. My

Gammy loves doing it." I had to get out of there. I wanted no part of her poisonous poultry or killer kebabs.

"Oh," Mrs. Zorch said, disappointed.

"I have something for you." I handed Zorch a letter. "Please take this."

Zorch furrowed his brow, confused. "What is it?"

"I can't say out loud. Just read it."

"This sounds dangerous, Austin," Zorch said.

"Please." I joked, "After all I've done for you?"

He didn't get it. "How many times have you almost blown up the school?" Zorch asked.

"Maybe a few times, but the key word is *almost*. Not *actually* blown up."

He weighed my wise retort.

I continued making my case. "I was the ring bearer at your wedding. I'm invoking ring-bearer rights." I didn't even know if that was a thing.

"Well, okay then."

Things just got serious.

THE GRADUATION CEREMONY HAD BEGUN. The eighth-grade graduating class was seated atop the auditorium stage with a few teachers and Ms. Pierre off to the side. Randy and I were behind the stage curtain, awaiting a special introduction as potential valedictorian candidates.

As outgoing president, Sophie led the attendees with the Pledge of Allegiance, a fine rendition, I must say, and then Dr. Dinkledorf, head of the Honors Society and student government programs, took the stage.

Randy sat next to me in his dorky gown and said, "I'm

gonna crush you, Davenfart. Here comes the final blow. You're goin' down."

"I'm going to forever call you number two once I win valedictorian," I said, while fixing my also-dorky gown.

My hand hit his, as I made the adjustments.

"Don't touch me, punk," Randy spat, disgusted. He used his forearm to push me away.

I rammed my shoulder into his, nearly knocking him off his chair.

He rammed me back, harder.

Dr. Dinkledorf's voice echoed throughout the auditorium, "These fine young men have dedicated their educational careers to excellence. I couldn't have asked for two finer young men to battle it out."

We apparently thought he meant literally. Randy stood up and kicked the side of my chair. I wobbled, trying to maintain my balance, but fell to the floor.

Dr. Dinkledorf continued, "Please welcome our valedictorian candidates!"

My anger clouded my judgement. Three years of frustration of being picked on and insulted by Randy bubbled over. I surged forward with Grimmwolf-like aggression, engulfing Randy in a savage tackle that would've made Mr. Muscalini proud. Randy back peddled, surprised by my unexpected attack, the momentum taking us through the curtains and onto the stage. We crashed to the ground, me on top of Randy. The entire crowd stared at us in silence. I looked up to a thousand eyeballs all on me. I didn't know what to do.

Mr. Muscalini broke the tension with an ear-curdling whistle. His voice bellowed, "Two points for the takedown! Go to a neutral corner and await my signal."

Randy pushed me off of him, and we both scrambled to our feet, which was quite difficult while wearing a flowing robe. Why did we have to look like such dweebs while graduating? I was used to it, but still.

Dr. Dinkledorf interjected. "Mr. Muscalini, this is not an MMA fight. Boys, take a seat. Now."

Randy and I did as we were told. The crowd groaned, apparently disappointed it was not an MMA fight. It would've been more exciting than what they were about to experience.

Mr. Muscalini looked at Ms. Pierre and said, "We gotta give the people what they want, right?"

"Sit down," Ms. Pierre said, furious.

"You look like a nun," Randy said to me.

"So do you, Sister Nancy!"

Dr. Dinkledorf said, "As C.T. Walsh once said, 'Great men make great entrances!' And what a great one that was. We have a few awards to give out. I reluctantly hand the microphone over to Mr. Muscalini."

Mr. Muscalini strode across the stage, his barreled chest leading the way. He stood in front of the podium and cleared his throat. "As you may know, I was once the county ping pong champion. I'm sure you can image the backhand I had with these triceps." He extended his arm and flexed his tri. "All you equestrian lovers out there, take a look at that horseshoe," he said, while staring at the bulging horse-shoe-shaped muscle on the back of his arm.

Somebody from the crowd yelled, "Let's go!"

"Oh, where was I? Oh, right. The glorious game of ping pong. But my experience was not so glorious. After winning the championship, I received no medal. No trophy. No ticker tape parade. I was devastated. I decided we would give out the biggest, baddest trophies that the world has ever seen. Speaking of biggest and baddest, have you seen my biceps?" Mr. Muscalini flexed. "Boom shockalacka. Or how about these quads? Bam, baby."

"Yo! Keep it moving."

"Right, so we have forty-seven athletic awards to hand out."

"We barely have forty-seven kids who play sports," somebody called out.

Mr. Muscalini called out every ridiculous award there was with a matching slide from his Powerpoint deck. Captains awards. Leadership awards. Losing with Honor awards. The Most Injured award. The Last Man Off The Bench award. It was ridiculous.

Mr. Muscalini said, "And now, for the final two awards.

The Student Athlete of the Year and Best Athlete of the Year."

I looked out into the crowd. Derek straightened up. I knew he was hoping to win Best Athlete.

Mr. Muscalini continued, "This year, these two accolades have been won by the same student."

I looked at my brother, knowing that he was not winning Student Athlete of the Year, but he was too stupid to realize. Ugh echoed throughout my being.

Randy stood up before his name was even called and patted me on the back. "Well on my way to the trifecta. Today is my day, Davenfart. Well, so is every day. You would think I would get bored being me, but I'm not."

"I'm certainly bored of you," I said.

"Randy Warblemacher!" Mr. Muscalini beamed.

My parents consoled the brooding Derek in the crowd. As much as I hated seeing Randy win, I'm a positive kinda guy. I focused on the silver lining and that was the fact that Derek lost. It's all about positive thinking, kids.

Dr. Dinkledorf walked up to the podium and said, "Enough pictures, you two. Sit down."

The two fame hounds did as they were told.

"Two more awards to go. The National Junior Honors Society Award for Student Excellence in Community Service or the NJHSASECS award as it's known in some circles, is given to, not surprisingly a National Junior Honors Society student who has shown excellence in community service.

Regan yelled out, "Snorefest, Dinkedork!"

Thankfully, he was old and didn't hear anything.

He continued, "This year's award goes to..." He opened the envelope and pulled out the card. "Cheryl Van Snoogle-Something!" The crowd cheered. "Ms. Van Snoogle-Something is an exemplary student and volunteers at a soup kitchen, a retirement home, and is a senior writer on our own Gopher Gazette! Congratulations to you, Ms. Van Snoogle-Something and to the entire Van Snoogle-Something family."

Cheryl nearly ran up on stage to accept the award. Rose Dumbleton looked like she was going to cry. Cheryl smiled at me and then for the camera, before heading back down.

"And now for our main event!" Dr. Dinkledorf said. He looked at Randy and me, concerned. "I don't mean that literally."

Dr. Dinkledorf paused for a moment, seemingly forgetting that hundreds of people were staring at him and had better things to do.

He looked over at Ms. Pierre and then back at the crowd. He said, "I've decided to switch things up. Please enjoy the unscripted portion of today's events."

Things had just gotten really interesting. Silence spread throughout the crowd. I glanced over at Ms. Armpit Hair, whose face registered concern.

Dr. Dinkledorf pulled out a letter from inside his suit jacket pocket. He adjusted the microphone and began reading, "Everyone has moments that define history. Not everyone's moments ripple throughout society and make the history books, but they are significant moments in that person's life and those around them. Today is one such day for me. It has been a pleasure to serve these students." He looked up at the crowd. "Today will be my last day."

Somebody yelled out, "You're dying today?"

Dr. Dinkledorf continued. "I am retiring from Cherry Avenue Middle School." He looked over at Ms. Armpit Hair. "Unfortunately, your regime does not allow us to serve, but to strike down students. Keep them in line. Pump them full of information like a giant balloon and then tie them down with rules until they pop."

I leaned over to Randy. "What the heck is he talking about?"

"If you were smart enough to be valedictorian, I wouldn't have to tell you."

I rolled my eyes and focused on Dr. Dinkledorf. He looked at the students and then into the crowd. "It has been my pleasure to serve you and those that came before you. I wish you the best in all your endeavors." He thrust his fist in the air and yelled, "Fight the power!"

The students burst out of their seats, and so did many of the parents, and some teachers in raucous applause. Dr. Dinkledorf then proceeded to trip over the podium, which knocked the mic to the ground. A screeching sound reverberated through the speakers. It was not the kind of mic drop most people look for, but still it was effective.

Dr. Dinkledorf walked through the crowd, shaking hands, as he made his way to the back of the auditorium.

I stood up and clapped. It was well deserved.

Ms. Pierre fixed the podium and then interrupted his farewell. "Well," she said into the microphone. "Good riddance. History can now move into the twenty-first century!"

Nobody had any idea what the heck she was talking about.

"Like all of it?" Randy asked.

"The true valedictorian would know the answer to that," I said, lying.

"I will announce the valedictorian." Ms. Armpit Hair took a deep breath and then tore open the envelope. She pulled it out slowly. She showed no emotion as she read the card to herself. My pulse pounded in my chest and my ears. Ms. Armpit Hair turned away from the microphone and said, "This year's eighth grade valedictorian is hwullah!"

"What? Who?" the crowd asked in confusion.

But I knew it was me! Only I could make Ms. Pierre puke like that.

Ms. Pierre took a deep breath and muttered into the microphone, "Austin Davenport."

"Yes! Yes!" I yelled, bursting out of my seat and breaking out into the Floss. I had no idea if that was still a valid dance move, but it felt right. "In your face, Nancy!"

Mr. Gifford yelled out, "The Love Doctor is in the house!"

My parents looked very confused.

The crowd went crazy. My parents and sister jumped up, clapping. Derek threw a fist in the air, but didn't get out of his seat. Typical. I couldn't believe that I had won. Well, I could. I'm a genius and all, but still. Randy usually cheated his way into victory when other people deserved it. I was still bitter about the sixth-grade science fair when he snowed everyone into believing that his robot was mind-controlled, but was instead controlled by one of his idiot friends with a video game controller under the table.

Ms. Pierre whispered into the microphone, "Mr. and Mrs. Davenport, please join me on the stage in presenting this hwullaward."

My parents bounced up onto the stage. My mother's huge belly didn't appear to slow her down. I stood there smiling, taking it all in, waiting for them to get to me on the stage. My Dad rushed forward and engulfed me in a hug.

"I'm so proud of you, Bud," he whispered, squeezing me tighter.

I said a muffled, "Thanks." And removed myself from his

sweaty armpit. I looked around him to see where my mother was.

She stood about six feet away, hunched over with her hands on her knees. Ahhhh, farts. It was her puke position. If only I could calm her down, I could save the day yet again, and avoid eternal shame in front of my peers. She grabbed her stomach and then returned her hands to her knees. She retched, but held it together.

I took two steps forward and realized I had moved in the wrong direction. She retched again. This time breakfast erupted from her mouth like a volcano. Kind of like the sixth-grade science fair volcano that destroyed my project. I'm sorry, but I apparently still have a fair (no pun intended) amount of unresolved issues relating to that day. Anyway, Mom opened her mouth and let out a auditorium-shaking, "Hwuuullllahh-hhh!" Slimy puke rocketed toward me like the speed of light. The hurl hurtled through the air, heading directly toward me.

Just Charles had once calculated that the average eighth-grade male nerd had been on the receiving end of no less than ten thousand dodgeballs rocketing toward him. My dodgeball instincts kicked in. I dove to my right, rolled in the air, landed on the hard stage with a smack, rolled again and stood up to a smattering of applause. But it wasn't finished. I teetered on the edge of the stage, slipped on a splatter of puke, and toppled down onto the floor below the stage.

Despite the fact that I nearly broke my face on the floor, I handled it quite well. One of the joys of being a nerd is you have a long list of embarrassing experiences to get you through the many new embarrassing experiences that you are bound to find yourself in or create. I had once tried to save a doll from falling off the stage in the middle of our middle school musical, slid off the stage, and you guessed it, nearly broke my face.

Anyway, back to the current face-breaking fall in front of a packed auditorium. Randy led the charge of laughter. He seems to believe that was his career. I hate to give the guy credit, but he's very good at it. He's got the pointing down. He's a pro at getting others to join in on the laughter. And he never lets you forget it.

Thunder rumbled inside the auditorium. I looked up in a daze to see Mr. Muscalini running through the crowd like a running back on Super Bowl Sunday, blasting unsuspecting middle schoolers with stiff arms and lowering his shoulders to plow over entire rows of kids.

"Don't worry! The Mus is coming!" he yelled. I worried what would happen when he arrived.

Mr. Muscalini hopped onto the stage like he was bouncing off a trampoline and then landed in a slick puddle of puke. He feet slipped out from underneath him as they touched down on the stage, and he slip-slided across six feet across the stage, knocking over one final victim. It was my favorite of the day. Ms. Armpit Hair. Her legs swept out from beneath her, she went horizontal, her evil head aiming for a collision with the hard wood floor. She put down her hand, lightning quick, seemingly about to pull out another one of her crazy ninja moves, but her hand did not find dry ground. Her palm slid across the floor, as her face connected with a knot in the wood beam.

Mr. Muscalini looked at his hands that were dripping with puke and for some unknown reason, decided to smell them. He promptly hurled, blasting a dazed and unsuspecting Principal Armpit Hair with a potent mix of half-digested beef jerky, chunks of chicken, and a strawberry protein shake sauce. Surprisingly, it looked a lot like the curious chicken from the cafeteria.

Before I knew it, Sophie and Ben were at my side, helping me to my feet, while holding their noses.

Mrs. Funderbunk stood atop the stage, in front of the podium. You never know what she's gonna say. I facepalmed myself, splattering puke everywhere.

"Ughhhh," Sophie said, seemingly about to puke.

Mrs. Funderbunk's voice boomed, "Good afternoon. Quite a turn of events here. But as they say in show biz, the show must go on! Everybody back to your places. Our valedictorian still has to give his speech. And if you'd like a season pass to next year's lineup of musicals and theatrical plays, please don't hesitate to order one at ayearoffunderbunk.com. Thank you!" She stepped to the side of the podium and took a bow like she had just given a Tony-Award-Winning performance.

There was a smattering of applause. Mr. Gifford led the charge and yelled, "That's my woman!" He grabbed a bouquet of flowers from the unsuspecting woman next to him and hurled (no pun intended, as far as you know) them up onto the stage.

Mrs. Funderbunk caught the flowers in midair, kicking her leg behind her like a movie star in a kissing scene, and then waved to the crowd like she had just won Miss America.

Zorch quickly mopped up the stage while those infected with puke took a few minutes to freshen up. First, I smelled like a walking fish filet. Now this.

I stood behind stage, not ready to go back out there and give a speech. I didn't really like speaking in front of large groups to begin with. I certainly didn't want to speak to this group after my mother had just puked on the stage all over me.

My mother wrapped her arm around me and whispered, "I'm so sorry. I know you can do this."

"Be strong," my father said. "You're a Davenport. We always get the job done."

I wasn't convinced of that. Maybe he was referring to those Davenports with the family butt chin, but I was not one of them.

My parents didn't even know what I was about to do. It was infinitely more difficult than a valedictorian speech. I was about to bring down one of the top agents from the C.I.A. or F.B.I.

I took a deep breath and walked out to the podium. There was another smattering of applause. People seemed disappointed that I didn't fall off the stage again.

I adjusted the mic lower. Somebody yelled, "Get the kid a step stool!"

I looked out at the crowd, wishing I had a diaper on. I looked over at Sophie. She nodded reassuringly.

"I, too, have a slide show presentation," I said into the microphone.

There was a smattering of boos. It took me what seemed like thirty minutes to find the entrance through my over-sized gown and into my pocket to retrieve the flash drive with my Pierre Prison Presentation.

Somebody called out, "What is he doing up there? The Macarena dance?"

I looked over to my friends for support. They all smiled. Sophie gave me a thumbs up. Just Charles cheersed me a brownie. I took a deep breath, fired up the presentation, and began.

"I'd like to thank Ms. Armpit Hair, I mean Ms. Ann Pierre, our esteemed principal for this award. After Prince Butt Hair, I figured we couldn't get any worse. I was wrong. Principal Buthaire and I never got along. But there is one thing I'm certain of. He would never steal from the school. Steal our freedom with eternal detention? Yes. Steal money. No. I can't say the same for Ms. Armpit Hair. We uncovered hundreds of international banking transactions to Cayman and Swiss banks that began once Ms. Pierre took over the school."

There were some cheers, a bunch of gasps of shock, but mostly stunned silence.

"My report can be downloaded at the website listed here," I said, pointing to the screen behind me.

Ms. Pierre stood on the stage, her hands balled in fists. "This is an outrage! This is preposterous!"

I yelled out to the crowd, "Arrest her!"

Nobody moved.

"Arrest her!" I repeated.

Ms. Armpit Hair smirked, stood up, and rushed for the exit with a cartwheel and a dive roll. It was totally unnecessary, but impressive, nonetheless. Perhaps I was just jealous at how well she executed a dive roll. In high heels, as usual. Not that I've ever wanted to dive roll in high heels. I can barely walk straight in sneakers. She probably should've saved those killer moves, though.

Amanda Gluskin had other ideas. If there were two people I wanted to see fight, it was the two of them. Ms. Armpit Hair had the training of an army ranger while Amanda was trained on the mean streets of Psychoville. It was gonna be a death match. I looked around for Zorch. He was the key to it all. And he was nowhere to be found. So much for ring bearer rights.

Amanda Gluskin surged forward. In one motion, Ms. Armpit Hair spun into Amanda's grasp, thrust her arm underneath Amanda's arm pit (fitting, I know), and used her leverage to flip Amanda over her shoulder. Amanda slammed into the wooden floor with a thwack and a groan. Even if we were wrong on Ms. Pierre stealing money, which we weren't, she had effectively just ended her principaling career, if that's such a thing. Most schools draw the line at performing advanced Judo on the children, no matter how wacky they were.

Ms. Pierre did a backwards roll away from Amanda and in one coordinated movement, rose to her feet like nothing had happened. Her smile turned to a frown as six police officers surged from behind the curtains with Zorch in the background. My letter! I knew Zorch would honor my ring bearer rights, even if it sounded like I doubted him just a few short seconds ago.

Without hesitation, Ms. Pierre reached into her pants suit jacket, retrieved something small, and slammed it onto the ground, just as the police swarmed her. With a poof, smoke billowed from the six-person pileup, unfortunately, with Ms. Pierre having gone poof herself.

I know what you're thinking. Oh. My. God. C.T. would be so excited! Yeah, but don't forget that my criminal principal just escaped.

I didn't know what to do. I looked to my friends for an idea. And that's when I saw Charles pop down another bite of brownie and bust through the chair-lined crowd in a blur.

Nobody knew where he was going, but I followed him, anyway. I rushed outside the auditorium into the Atrium with Sophie, Ben, Sammie, Cheryl, and Luke at my heels. It was chaos. Mayhem, even, as the crowd flowed into the Atrium like a giant ocean wave.

When I arrived in the Atrium, I didn't know what to make of what I saw. Ms. Pierre was out cold, sprawled out in a most uncomfortable position, which seemed to indicate multiple broken bones. Just Charles was sitting on top of Ms. Pierre's butt, munching on some cookies that he must've grabbed either before or after his takedown/breakdown of Ms. Armpit Hair.

Just Charles saw us and bounced up like he had butt springs or an ejector seat, his sugar rush kicking in to complete his villainous transformation. He yelled, "Evil-Chucksavedtheday!"

A CROWD LINED the Atrium wall that led to the exit doors. I stood with my parents and my crew watching as a female police officer led Ms. Pierre on a stretcher wheeled by a portly EMT. Both of Ms. Pierre's wrists were handcuffed to the sides of the stretcher. She fought the restraints, to no avail. Even with her skills, she was no match for metal.

"What do you think will happen?" I asked my father.

Dad said, "She'll go to a white collar prison, start a gang, and be running the place in no time."

"She might escape," Derek added, unhelpfully. "Fueled with rage, she'll want revenge and kill you in your sleep."

"Well, thanks to you, *I* won't be sleeping for quite some time," I said.

As the crowd dwindled in the Atrium, I said my good-byes to my friends, and was about to head over to my parents, who were speaking to Mrs. Trugman, my mother's friend, when I heard a slow, patronizing clap. I turned to see none other than the Prince of Butt Hair, my high school principal. He stood in the shadows, as he finished his clap. "Well played. I may have underestimated you."

"Thank you?" I said, not really sure how to answer that.

Principal Buthaire stepped forward. "You know, you and I aren't so different. Except for that fish smell. God, where did you get that?"

"Dang it! I thought it was gone."

Principal Butt Hair continued, "You have a choice, Austin."

He called me Austin. He never does that. It's usually a drawn-out Misterrrrr Davenport.

His eyes widened and wry smile emerged on his face. "Join me and we can rule high school together!" He finished with his signature high-pitched cackle.

"Can you use a deep voice, a lot lower than your whiny voice, and say, 'Join me on the dark side?'"

"Whiny voice?" he whined. "No. I won't say that," he said, straining his voice lower.

"Okay," I shrugged. I didn't let him kill the moment. I yelled back, "Never! I will not join the dark side!"

Prince Butt Hair twisted his bushy mustache, as he glared at me. "Very well, Misterrrr Davenport. Very well. Enjoy your summer. Because when the school year arrives, your butt is mine."

I grabbed my cheeks behind me, protectively. "I'd very much like to keep my butt, sir. And that's kinda weird. I should tell my parents, I think."

"No, don't do that. I just meant I'm gonna make your life miserable."

"Oh, okay. There's nothing weird about a principal telling the incoming valedictorian that," I said.

"I'll be waiting for you," he said, again forcing his voice lower. He turned and disappeared into the shadows.

"I can't wait for you to wait!" I said, and then muttered to myself. "Not a bad exit, I must say, but it would've been a lot cooler with a smoke bomb."

20

I sat on the couch in my den, waiting for Sammie's graduation party to start. I read C.T. Walsh's newest blockbuster while my dad watched the news.

I looked up when I heard Calvin Conklin's voice. Calvin sat at the news desk with Sara Keane, his co-anchor. Calvin said, "Disgraced principal Ann Pierre is behind bars after a bizarre alleged embezzling accusation by none other than a group of middle school sleuths."

"Everybody, get in here!" Dad yelled.

My mother, brother, and sister all entered the den and stood behind the couch.

"They're talking about Armpit Hair," I said.

"That's right, Calvin. A group of her own students uncovered the plot and turned her in, in grand fashion."

"Cherry Avenue Middle School's valedictorian spilled the beans," Calvin said. He turned to Sara and asked, "You know what they say about beans, don't you?" He pressed his earpiece. "Sorry, Ted. But can we sing the Beans song after? Okay." Calvin looked back at the camera and said, somewhat disappointed, "During the boy genius' speech-"

"Boy genius!" I yelled.

"Whatever," Derek said.

Calvin continued, "He outed the felonious administrator. It took multiple students to take her down, but in the end, the students saved the day. And now, we're hearing reports that Ann Pierre is really Li Yun, a spy who had been excommunicated by China's secret police unit."

"I knew it!" I yelled.

"That's crazy," my father said.

"Whatever," Derek said, again.

"Your vocabulary range is exquisite," I said. "Is that toddler level?"

"Shut up," Derek said.

My mother looked at me. "You should head over to the graduation party. You don't want Sammie to get angry."

I looked at Derek and asked, "You going?"

"Yeah. As long as Randy wasn't invited," Derek said.

"Nope." Sammie had been over Randy for quite some time.

"Good."

"Let's go," I said, popping up.

I STOOD WITH BEN, Sammie, and Luke, waiting for Sophie and the rest of our crew to arrive. We stood by the snacks (what else is new?) and checked out the rest of the attendees. A bunch of my friends were there. Jimmy Trugman, Jay Parnell, Barn Door, and even Max. I wondered how Sammie knew him or if he had been hired to run the bathroom by the pool house.

I took a deep breath when Amanda Gluskin walked in.

"What is she doing here?" I asked.

"Somebody's getting their butt kicked tonight," Luke said.

"It just might be you," Just Charles said.

"None of us are safe," I said. "I'm surprised she's even here after she got blasted by Armpit Hair," I said.

"She probably wants to regain her confidence by bullying the rest of us," Ben said.

"I didn't invite her," Sammie said, confused.

"Why would you? You only invite her if you want to get glitter bombed," I said, remembering the 'present' she left for me at the science fair, which blew a butt ton of glitter up my nose. I may or may not have misled her about my brother and I wanting to date her. It was not one of my finer moments. She repaid me with a faux present, which upon opening, blasted my face with glitter. I did have the best-looking snot around for the next few weeks. My parents were so proud.

"She has a present," Luke said. "How nice."

I turned away from her, still not sure where we stood after I had called her a psycho and she almost separated my head from my body.

"Don't open it," I said to Sammie. "I'm pretty certain it's a glitter bomb."

"Thanks for the tip," she said.

Ben scratched his head and asked, "What did you do to deserve that?"

"She blamed a fart on me in gym class and I denied it."

"How is that your problem?" I asked.

"Tell me about it," Sammie said.

"She should've done what C.T. does- blame it on a barking tree frog," I said.

Sammie asked, "Are they often found in the gymnasium?"

Just Charles said, "They're found wherever one is needed."

"Aaaahhhh, farts," I said.

Randy Warblemacher entered the backyard with the hulking Nick DeRozan by his side. Randy's smirk was particularly over the top. I would've thought that with the valedictorian loss, he would've been less smirky, but I guess his crashing the party was his way of thinking he was cool again. The fact that he wasn't invited to the party probably should've given him the hint that he was, in fact, not cool, but who am I to judge the complexities of the inhuman middle schooler?

I locked eyes with Randy. His smirk disappeared. But not in a good way. His face morphed into anger. Hatred, even. And it was all directed at me. Randy pounded his fist in his hand and nodded to Nick. Randy wasn't there to regain his jerkiness by crashing a party. He was there to kick my butt.

"Uh, oh," I said. "Where's Derek?" It pained me that my first thought was of my brother's location.

"I don't see him," Ben said.

Just Charles said, "You realize there is only a ten percent chance your brother helps you, forty percent chance he watches you get your butt kicked, and a fifty percent chance that he also kicks your butt?"

"I'm hoping for that ten percent," I said.

Randy was closing in on me. "Davenfart, time to talk! With our fists!"

"What now?" Luke asked.

I know what you're probably thinking. After everything Austin has endured over the past three years with Randy, Derek, Principals Butt Hair and Armpit Hair, the Pretty Posse, and natural disasters, it's finally his moment to stand tall, become a man, and fight Randy like the forces of good and evil intended. You would be wrong.

I answered Luke's question, "Our best bet would be to... ruuuuuuunnnnnn!" I took off running, hopped off the deck, promptly fell, but looked cool rolling across the grass. I jumped up, exhausted. If you don't know I'm a nerd by now, I don't know what to tell you.

I bounced up and headed toward the fence on the other side of the house. Randy might have speed, but I had knowledge. I knew Sammie's land like the back of my hand. I had grown up next door to her. The fact that it was less than half an acre meant that advantage was not all that significant, particularly when Randy could run across the entire property in ten seconds, but still.

I cut around the side of the house, knowing my window of opportunity was only a few seconds. I was out of sight of all the guests. I pulled open the gate. It swung open with a clank. But instead of running through it, which would surely result in Randy tracking me down and implementing the Camel Clutch on the front lawn for all my neighbors and Sammie's guests to see, I hopped into the bushes on the side of the house inside the gate.

I yelped as forty million sharp objects punctured every millimeter of my epidermis, and then held my breath. Randy sped by and out through the gate. The lumbering steps of Nick DeRozan weren't far behind.

Randy's curses echoed off the aluminum siding. My friends and most of the remaining guests funneled out into the front yard.

"Did you know Davenfart was that fast?" Randy asked.

Nick's deep voice answered, "No, but you *were* going to pummel him."

Randy corrected Nick, "I *am* going to pummel him. He's probably crying to his mommy." Randy laughed.

I peeked out through the bushes to see Sammie push Randy on the chest with both hands. I gently bit my finger to avoid yelling.

"Get out of here! I hate you!" Sammie yelled.

Randy laughed. "Chill out, Sammie. I thought you were cool."

"If being cool means I'm okay with you crashing my party and beating up my friend, then no. Get out."

Randy looked at Nick and said, "Let's get out of here. This is a nerd party anyway."

I waited for Randy to leave and the rest of the crowd to return to the party. I hobbled my way back to my house, walked in the door, and yelled a manly, "Mommy!"

My mother shuffled into the foyer, her belly beating her into the room by a good two seconds.

"What happened?" she asked, looking horrified that her baby boy had become a walking pin cushion.

"Oh, my goodness. I'll be right back."

I texted my friends, alerting them to my less-than-well-being while my mother got tweezers. Lucky me.

To add insult to injury, I spent the next half hour watching TV in my room while my mother plucked thorns out of my butt cheeks. But at least I got to catch up on my Spanish soap operas. I could not believe that Jorge stopped loving Adrianna. He was just hurt because he found that old letter she sent to a former lover. It was a simple misunderstanding. But I knew they would work it out after some fireworks.

Anyway, Sophie and Just Charles waited in the den with my sister, waiting for me to recover. Well, it was actually just more injury. They hurt as much on the way out as on the way in.

Finally, I gingerly walked into the den. My sister looked up and said, "All good, butt boy?"

Sophie asked, "Are you okay?"

"Just great," I said, sarcastically. "I ran away from a fight in front of half the school and then had my mom pluck thorns out of my butt cheeks for the last half hour."

My dad said, "I don't really know what to say about the butt plucking, but there's nothing wrong with running away from a fight. Some fights are worth it. Some aren't. Fighting with Randy because he's angry you beat him as valedictorian is not worth it."

"Yeah, but it's so much more than that. It's been three years of this. He needs to get his butt kicked. I'd rather take that 1% chance the sun gets in his eyes while I swing a folding chair at his head, with the 99% likelihood that get beat up, rather than be a coward," I said.

"I actually calculate your odds of getting beat up at 99.9%," Just Charles said.

I glared at him.

"But close enough," Just Charles said.

"I should just give you some sugar and let you beat him up," I said, laughing.

Just Charles shrugged. "Cheryl made me swear off sugar."

My mom chimed in, "Fighting's not the answer. It's over. Summer's here. You won't see him in school and you'll start fresh in the fall in high school."

"I guess you're right. I just wish somebody would kick his butt," I said.

Everybody laughed.

"Do you want to go back to the party?" Sophie asked. "We don't have to."

I took a deep breath. I didn't want to look at anyone, but I didn't want to disappoint Sammie, either. "We can go back," I said, trying to sound excited. "As long as you're okay with me standing up. For the next week. And hiding in the corner."

"Yeah, Sophie, keep your hands off my son's butt," my father said.

Sophie's face went red.

My mother smacked my father's arm.

"Sorry," my father said, sheepishly.

TWO MINUTES after I walked into Sammie's backyard, I immediately regretted it. I walked up toward the food table, about to grab a cheeseburger, when I heard the familiar voice of Randy Warblemacher, "Well, the coward returns," Randy said from behind me.

I turned around. "Why? Why can't I ever get a break?"

Randy wore a baseball hat, pulled down so low, it covered his eyebrows. He was so tall, it didn't really conceal his identity, because we all look up at his face. But I guess when you're not valedictorian, those things don't occur to you.

"Just leave, Randy. Nobody wants you here," Sophie said, angrily.

I took a step to the side, attempting to get around Randy, but he quickly shuffled in front of me. Nick DeRozan walked up behind Randy.

"There's no escape now, Davenport. I knew you would fall for my trap," Randy said with his signature smirk.

"What makes you think you didn't fall for mine?" I asked, forcing a chuckle, knowing I had no plan whatsoever, excluding eating that tasty burger.

"Does your trap involve you getting punched in the face after I wait for you to come back to the party?"

"No. No, it doesn't," I said, concerned.

"Then I didn't fall into your trap."

"Maybe," I said, stalling.

Randy pounded his fist into his other hand. "I'm gonna kick your butt."

"Please don't. For reasons I don't really want to get into right now."

A crowd started to gather. Derek pushed his way through, never one to miss a good bashing, if he wasn't the one giving it. Derek's arrival could go either way for me. He could punch me in the face first, not wanting Randy to beat him to it, or he could back me up. So, I was pretty much about to get punched in the face. Maybe twice.

I flinched as Derek stopped next to me. The punch never arrived.

Derek looked at Randy and said, "Enough, Warblemacher. You have a problem with him, you have a problem with me. And I'm not a nerd."

I could've done without the last part, but I let it slide. I beamed with pride. My big brother, even though he was a measly eleven months older than me, had finally stood up for me. Took ya long enough, bro.

My valedictorian senses left me. Or did they? I stepped forward and said to Derek, "I got this, bro. But thank you. I'll take my beating and be done with it."

"Austin, no!" Sophie said, but Luke held her back.

"He's got that look in his eye," Luke said. "Like when he crushed Amy Howard in chess in third grade."

Crushing that pretentious Amy Howard *was* one of my finest moments, but I didn't see how a strategy game of the mind had anything to do with wrestling with the best athlete in the school, if not the county. Or did it?

"At least you're self-aware, Davenfart," Randy said.

I whispered to Derek, "Just stop it before it gets out of hand."

"Okay. I'll wait until your unconscious."

I nodded. "Okay. Thanks. Wait? What? No! Sooner than that."

Derek shrugged, noncommittally. "I'll see how it goes. Now get out there and crush him! You don't have the Davenport chin, but I almost believe in you," Derek said, pushing me toward Randy.

Max yelled out, "Aus the Boss! You've got this. Remember The Thing!"

The Thing. The Thing! I felt a surge of energy rush through me. Max had once hypnotized me to take Randy's medieval beating by pretending I was the rock-like mutant, The Thing, from the Fantastic Four.

And then Luke yelled out, "Remember Amy Howard!"

Ditzy Dayna followed with, "Is this a dance off? I love those!"

I ignored Dayna's dumbness as Randy and I circled each other, looking for a weakness. And then Amy Howard popped into my head. Chess. You have to be thinking three moves ahead to beat a great player. I had zero moves planned, so I was in trouble.

Before I could think of anything to do, Randy pounced on me with lighting quickness, his strength and momentum, pushing me backward. We stumbled over toward the food table in a strange sort of angry hug, each of us trying to body slam the other. I butt bumped the table. It clanked and then flipped over, spring rolls springing and/or rolling and cheese whiz whizzing in all directions. As I crashed down on top of the table, Randy on top of me, a vegetable tray rained down on us. It was like Cloudy with a Chance of Meatballs, only not nearly as fun. And surely not to have a happy ending for me. Carrots are good for your eyes, except when they are poking you in them.

"Owww!" I yelled.

"You're such a baby, Davenfart," Randy said in my ear, grappling with me. "It's just broccoli." His breath was worse than a punch to my face.

"I was owwing because of the brick in my back," I said, crawling away from him.

"Oh, yeah. That hurts."

I winced. "And easy on the onion dip, bro! Your breath is on the attack!"

I slithered away, a skill I had learned from many years of abuse from Derek, and got to me feet. Randy was still behind me, so I didn't want to go that way, but I was blocked by the present table. I had no interest in more tables. But then I had an idea. Presents! I scanned the table, as I surged toward it. I had a mind-blowing chess move that Randy didn't know existed.

Randy wrapped his arms around me from behind. I reached out my hand and grabbed Amanda Gluskin's present. Before Randy bounced me on the deck like a basketball.

I was on my stomach with Randy sitting on my back, attempting to implement the dreaded Camel Clutch on me in front of my girlfriend and all of my peers. He slipped his hands underneath my chin, about to clasp his fingers together, before implementing the devastating camel pose by pulling up. I bit his hand.

Randy shrieked in pain. The crowd cheered. I used both hands in front of me to attempt to pop the top of Amanda's present, unleashing my own devastating move. The Glitter Bomb. Randy had shaken off my ferocious bite, which I had perfected over many years of being pummeled by Derek, and was back to working his fingers together for the inevitable Camel Clutch.

"You've got to stop this thing!" Sophie yelled to Derek.

"No, he's not getting beat. He's gonna win this thing!" Derek yelled. I had never heard him so excited over one of my triumphs. I wasn't anywhere close to an actual triumph, though. But still. It was a nice sentiment.

I gasped for air as the pressure from Randy on my back weighed on my chest, not to mention the struggle against the Camel Clutch. I could feel Randy's hands getting closer together, despite my constant nipping at his fingers like a savage dog.

Randy yelled out, "Got you, sucka!"

I used all of my strength to roll to my side, taking Randy with me. I popped the top of the Glitter Bomb, which promptly exploded in Randy's face. Glitter blasted his very-surprised and not-so-smug face. And pretty much everything else in a five-foot radius.

Randy shrieked in pain and fell to his stomach, grabbing his eyes. I needed to finish him. I hopped on top of Randy, easily slipped and clasped my fingers beneath his chin, and leaned back, executing the emotionally and spiritually draining Camel Clutch with perfection. I held it for a short second, just to make sure everyone saw. And then Randy pounded his palm on the deck.

"He's tapping out!" Derek yelled.

I let go of Randy and rolled off him to stunned silence.

Randy rolled to his side and then proceeded to cough up some of the prettiest puke I've ever seen. I mean, I hate the guy, but it was downright beautiful.

I sat up, my chest still heaving. I couldn't believe that I had beaten Randy in a physical fight. The entire crowd was shocked. Nobody knew what to say or do. We all just watched Randy deal with the glitter.

"My eyes. My eyes," he whined.

Regan rushed to his side. "My baby!"

Luke was the first to break the silence like a boxing ring announcer. He raised my arm into the air. "Austiiiiiiiin Davennnnnport! Lehhhhhhgend!"

The crowd erupted into cheers. Sophie, Ben, Sammie, and just about everyone else there rushed forward into a giant hug. After a few minutes of celebration, things settled down.

Derek pat me on the back. "That was incredible," he said.

"Unreal," Ben added.

Just Charles said, "I could've done that with a little sugar."

I chuckled.

Sophie asked, "Are you okay?"

"I'm amazing," I said. "But you already know that."

Sophie smirked, then laughed.

Ditzy Dayna looked at me and said, "Austin, you look like a unicorn puked on you."

"Thanks," I said, sarcastically. At least she got my name right.

And then Kami Rahm said, "Look at Randy. Oh my God, he's sparkling. He looks so hot."

A bunch of girls fainted.

Ahhh, farts.

WELL, there you have it. That was middle school for me and my crew. If there is one word to describe it, well, besides flatulence, it would be mayhem. And a lot of it. I had endured so much, but at that moment, it was all worth it.

Now I'm off to high school, which I will surely chronicle for your enjoyment. Based on my middle school experience, it's bound to be high school hysteria.

WANT FREE STUFF?

CHARACTER INTERVIEWS?

ACTIVITY SHEETS?

SHORT STORIES?

DISCOUNTED BOOKS?

OTHER BONUSES?

C.T.'S MONTHLY NEWSLETTER?

OF COURSE, YOU DO!

ctwalsh.fun/msmbonuses

Got Audio?

Want to listen to Middle School Mayhem?

A NOTE FROM C.T.

You made it! Thank you for being a part of Nerd Nation! You completed the most fartastic middle school adventure in the history of the world. Is that really true? I mean, it hasn't been authenticated by a government agency, but I think it's pretty obvious, no?

Anyway, I hope you enjoyed reading Austin's wild adventures as much as I enjoyed writing them. I wrote all twelve books (that's a lot of mayhem!) in three years and published them all in less than two years, which was a lot of hard work, so it gives me great pleasure to know that you took this journey with me.

For now, Austin is tired of me following him around chronicling (is that a word?) his every move. He was like, "C.T., dude. How do you know my brother combs his armpit hair? And you're selling my stories? I want a cut of that. M.I.T. isn't gonna be cheap. Send a contract to Max and I may consider telling you my high school adventures."

So, until my people work things out with his people, we're on hold for more stories, but I have a feeling we will come to an agreement at some point. Until then, happy reading and thanks again for being a part of Middle School Mayhem!

ABOUT THE AUTHOR

C.T. Walsh is the author of the Middle School Mayhem Series, which is a total twelve hilarious adventures of Austin Davenport and his friends. He also has four picture books for younger readers with many more to come.

Besides writing fun, snarky humor and the occasionally-frequent fart joke, C.T. loves spending time with his family, coaching his kids' various sports, and successfully turning seemingly unsandwichable things into spectacular sand-wiches, while also claiming that he never eats carbs. He assures you, it's not easy to do. C.T. knows what you're think-ing: this guy sounds complex, a little bit mysterious, and maybe even dashingly handsome, if you haven't been to the optometrist in a while. And you might be right.

C.T. finds it weird to write about himself in the third person, so he is going to stop doing that now.

You can learn more about C.T. (oops) at ctwalsh.fun

 facebook.com/ctwalshauthor

ALSO BY C.T. WALSH

Middle School Mayhem Series

Down with the Dance: Book One

Santukkah!: Book Two

The Science (Un)Fair: Book Three

Battle of the Bands: Book Four

Medieval Mayhem: Book Five

The Takedown: Book Six

Valentine's Duh: Book Seven

The Comic Con: Book Eight

Election Misdirection: Book Nine

Education Domestication: Book Ten

Class Tripped: Book Eleven

Picture Books

The 250-Year-Old Bride

The Kung Pao Cow

Who Hides Under Monsters' Beds?

What Do Monsters Eat & Drink?

Backwards Bogart

Made in the USA
Columbia, SC
16 November 2020

24705225R00120